"Your grandfa[ther was in] the state penite[ntiary for] the past seven ye[ars."]

Evan was obviously putting two and two together.

"He will never steal anything again," Alexandra said forcefully, rather than answer his questions. "Do you know what his time in prison did to his dignity? It isn't something he would ever chance having happen again."

Alexandra stared at Evan, seeing his doubts as clearly as she'd seen them in other people all her life.

"In case you're wondering," she said ruefully, "I've never stolen a thing in my life."

Evan gave a humorless little chuckle at that and pushed off the railing. He came to sit beside her, taking her hands in his and looking at them, his expression sober. "Yes, you have. I think you've stolen my heart, Alexandra."

Dear Reader,

Welcome to Silhouette **Special Edition**... welcome to romance. Each month, Silhouette **Special Edition** publishes six novels with you in mind—stories of love and life, tales that you can identify with—romance with that little "something special" added in.

This month, Silhouette **Special Edition** is full of special treats for you. We're hosting Nora Roberts's third book in her exciting THE CALHOUN WOMEN series—*For the Love of Lilah*. Each line at Silhouette Books has published one book of the series. Next month look for *Suzanna's Surrender* in the Silhouette Intimate Moments line!

Silhouette **Special Edition** readers are also looking forward to the second book in the compelling SONNY'S GIRLS series, *Don't Look Back* by Celeste Hamilton. These poignant tales are sure to be keepers! Don't miss the third installment next month, *Longer Than...* by Erica Spindler.

Rounding out August are warm, wonderful stories by veteran authors Sondra Stanford, Karen Keast and Victoria Pade, as well as Kim Cates's wonderful debut book, *The Wishing Tree*.

In each Silhouette **Special Edition**, we're dedicated to bringing you the romances that you dream about—the type of stories that delight as well as bring a tear to the eye. And that's what Silhouette **Special Edition** is all about—special books by special authors for special readers!

I hope you enjoy this book and all of the stories to come.

Sincerely,

Tara Gavin
Senior Editor

VICTORIA PADE
The Right Time

Silhouette Special Edition

Published by Silhouette Books New York

America's Publisher of Contemporary Romance

To the Ashley Allyn in my family, with love

SILHOUETTE BOOKS
300 East 42nd St., New York, N.Y. 10017

THE RIGHT TIME

ISBN: 0-373-09689-5

First Silhouette Books printing August 1991

Printed in the U.S.A.

Books by Victoria Pade

Silhouette Special Edition

Breaking Every Rule #402
Divine Decadence #473
Shades and Shadows #502
Shelter from the Storm #527
Twice Shy #558
Something Special #600
Out on a Limb #629
The Right Time #689

VICTORIA PADE,

bestselling author of both historical and contemporary romance fiction, is the mother of two energetic daughters, Cori and Erin. Although she enjoys her chosen career as a novelist, she occasionally laments that she has never traveled farther from her Colorado home than Disneyland, instead, spending all her spare time plugging away at her computer. She takes breaks from writing by indulging in her favorite hobby—eating chocolate.

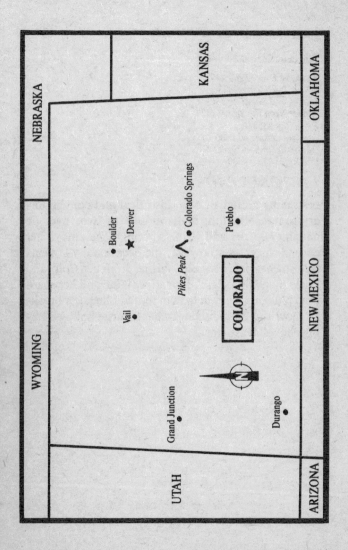

Chapter One

"Lift your right foot, Alexandra. Good. Now your left."

Alexandra Dunbar did as her grandfather instructed, paying more attention to the papers she was gathering to put inside her briefcase. But when he caught the pant leg of her gray wool slacks in the vacuum cleaner's nozzle, she glanced sharply at the eighty-two-year-old man kneeling just behind her, as he tried to clean under her desk. Ah, the complications of running a business out of one's home! she mused.

"You had a piece of string on your cuff," her grandfather explained without looking up at her.

"Couldn't this wait until I'm gone, Tommy?" she said in a voice loud enough to be heard over the machine's noise.

Tommy Dewberry flipped off the machine's switch. "Did you say something?" he asked with a grin that made his pale blue eyes sparkle.

"This appointment is really important. Don't you think this could wait until I get everything I need and leave?" Then on second thought she suggested, "Or, you could just relax in front of the television and I'll do the cleaning later."

"Now, how could I do that?" he asked as he got agilely to his feet and perched on the edge of her desk like a debonair leprechaun. He wore brown slacks, a white dress shirt and a red silk scarf tied around his neck, the knot at a jaunty angle. "Here you are, putting a roof over my head, providing three square meals a day and refusing to take a penny from me. How could I sit and watch TV while the dust piles up waiting for you to do the cleaning, too?"

Barely five feet tall, Tommy was a hundred and thirty pounds of charm, and Alexandra was anything but immune to it. She couldn't help smiling at him. "Besides, you couldn't stand to leave a speck of dust anywhere."

He winked at her. "That, too, darling. That, too."

"Okay, then. Could you just let me get my stuff together and get out of here before you sterilize my desk?"

Tommy threw his long-fingered hands into the air, palms outward. "I won't touch a thing until you're gone." And he sat motionless while Alexandra searched for a particular brochure.

"Where is the information on that new laser alarm?" she muttered to herself.

"Is this what you're looking for?" he asked, pointing to a corner that peeked out from under the contracts she had set in her briefcase just before he'd vacuumed her ankle.

"Oh, good. I was afraid I'd lost it again. Except that I didn't lose it yesterday. You moved it when you were cleaning. And if you cleaned yesterday, why are you cleaning again today?"

"Keep a tidy ship, Alexandra," he recited.

She rolled her eyes. If she'd heard him say that once in her life she'd heard him say it a gazillion times—along with any number of other adages he quoted for every occasion. "'Tidy' is one thing. 'Immaculate' is something else," she pointed out.

"Yes, it is. It's better." His grin was infectious and Alexandra couldn't help returning it with a shake of her head. Then Tommy changed the subject. "This must be an important job. You seem awfully tense about it."

Important certainly was the word. Buying her first house so that she would have a place to bring Tommy to live, a yard he could garden and roots for them both, had put much more strain on Alexandra's finances than she'd expected. And since her business, Security Systems, had been in operation barely a year, it was not a good time for added expenses. A contract to install a sensitive, high-tech alarm system to protect the private collection of one of Denver's wealthy new residents was just what the doctor ordered. But since the last thing she wanted Tommy to know was that his being with her had put her in a money crunch she said, "All jobs are important."

"Well, if the guy takes one look at you and doesn't hire you on the spot, he's crazy and we don't want him."

"You're good for my ego. Even if you do have a biased opinion," she told him as she closed her briefcase and headed out.

Her office was separated from her bedroom by a bathroom. She stopped there to make a last check on her appearance in the mirror over the sink.

The gray wool pinstripe was her lucky suit, and the high-necked white silk blouse she wore underneath softened its tailored lines. Very light makeup—just enough blush to enhance her cheekbones, and a little mascara to darken the lashes of the blue eyes she'd inherited from Tommy—and her light reddish hair tied in a loose knot halfway down its waist length, tempered her professional ensemble with the right touch of femininity. Just the image she wanted.

"Here, you need this," Tommy spoke up from the doorway. He untied the red silk scarf from around his neck and stuffed it in her breast pocket with his own special brand of panache. "Perfect. Now just hold on and I'll go get your shoes. They're down in my bedroom. I polished them this morning."

"They've only been worn once. There wasn't anything to polish," Alexandra said as she followed her grandfather through the living room into the kitchen.

"Shoes should shine like mirrors," he recited.

"You have to be the biggest neatnik I've ever known, T. C. Dewberry."

"At your service," he replied, bowing low over his arm before he went down the stairs that led off the kitchen.

The basement was part of the reason Alexandra had overextended herself to buy this particular house. It was actually a complete apartment with a bedroom, living room, bath and kitchen. Tommy used the main kitchen but if he wanted, he could stay downstairs, coming and going as he pleased through the back door without so much as even running into Alexandra.

He was back upstairs almost before she'd had time to put her briefcase on the round pedestal table. "How about tacos for dinner tonight? They're number ten on the list," he said as she slipped on her shoes.

"That's fine," Alexandra agreed, knowing the list to be a seven-year compilation of foods Tommy missed while he'd been away. Had he been back with her for ten days already? It seemed like only yesterday. She tucked her briefcase under her arm, slung her purse over her shoulder and kissed him on the cheek. "I'm so glad you're here," she said impulsively.

"No happier than I am, darling," he answered. Then, smoothing a palm over his bald head and down the back to his neck, he added, "What do you say you give me a little trim tonight after dinner?"

"Your fringe is getting long, all right," she remarked facetiously. "It almost touches your collar. Want me to bring home a little glue and we'll see if we can get what I cut off to stick to the top"

"And ruin my high-brow profile? I don't think so."

"I remember when Grandma would make you sit on the floor in front of her so she could use that electric massager on the top of your head. She was convinced it would make you grow new hair," Alexandra said, laughing.

"It's a wonder she didn't shake my brains into mush with that thing," he remarked with so much affection, Alexandra knew he'd enjoyed the attention. But then there was no doubt about how much he had loved her grandmother, and Alexandra couldn't help wondering if anyone would ever love her the way Tommy had loved Rose.

"Well, I'd better get going," she said, shaking herself out of her thoughts. "Take some time for yourself this afternoon, will you? Don't clean all day."

Tommy shooed her away. "Go get your job and leave this place to a pro. I've had too much time to myself for the past seven years."

"How about a nap, then? I don't want you to wear yourself out. You aren't a spring chicken anymore, you know."

"I've had more than enough naps, too. Now, go on and quit worrying about me."

Alexandra kissed his cheek once more. "I like worrying about you," she told him as she headed for the door.

It was a bright October day; autumn was in the crispness of the air but the sun was warm. In the driveway, leaves the color of flame had fallen from her neighbor's oak tree onto the hood of her tan station wagon and they crackled under the tires of the truck that was just pulling up to the curb in front of her house.

Alexandra checked her watch. She had a few minutes to spare, so she set her purse and briefcase on the car seat and waited for John Rodaway to get out of his truck.

Three years older than her own thirty-five, John was a childhood friend who had settled in Colorado along with Alexandra and Tommy. Over the years he'd kept in touch with both of them, and when Alexandra had started Security Systems he'd agreed to work for the fledgling company.

"How did it go?" Alexandra asked as the tall blond came up to her car.

John shook his head. "We were outbid by a larger company."

"Damn."

"I'm sorry. But it wasn't much of a job, anyway, Alexandra. A bottom-of-the-line system for a small shop."

"I know," she said quickly. If anyone should be apologizing it was herself. Within two weeks of buying her house, business had slowed to a snail's crawl. It was one thing to cut her own salary, but John had been accepting whatever portion of his installer's wages she could scrape together, too.

"You'll have better luck with this appointment today," he reassured her. "Besides, riding these ups and downs is all worth it to have your own company. If I were you I'd be so glad of that, I wouldn't sweat the small stuff."

"You're right," she agreed rather than pointing out that even the "small stuff" made a profit. "Hey, in case I haven't told you lately, you're really a good friend, to both Tommy and me. I appreciate that you keep sticking with us through the rough patches." She bit her tongue before telling him yet again that she hadn't forgotten the money she owed him. It only embarrassed him and it didn't do anything to lessen the guilt she felt. Instead she said, "I hope Tommy isn't bending your ear too much. It seems like he nabs you every time you come in."

John turned his face up to the early-afternoon sun, squinting his brown eyes. "I've always liked talking to Tommy. There's never a dull moment with him. And he doesn't talk all that much," John added.

That made Alexandra laugh. ''Tommy? Who are you trying to kid? My grandfather can talk circles around a filibustering politician.''

"It's okay. I don't mind," John insisted again. "You better get to that appointment. You don't want to look bad by being late."

"True." Alexandra got into her car, closed the door and rolled down the window. "Tommy is fixing tacos for dinner tonight. If you're not busy, why don't you stay?"

John grinned. "I'd like to but I have a date."

"Again?" she teased in an exaggerated tone of voice.

"Yeah, again."

"Same lady?"

"Yeah." He blushed.

"It must be serious."

He shrugged like an embarrassed kid. "Only if I'm a lucky man."

"Don't doubt yourself for a minute," she said as if she were reassuring a brother. "She'd be the lucky one to get you."

He grinned. "Think so?"

Alexandra gave him the once-over. "Blond as a beach boy, killer green eyes, perfect white teeth and a body honed at an early age by the T. C. Dewberry regimen? You bet."

John just laughed and blushed to an even deeper crimson. "Thanks." He cleared his throat. "If I'm not here when you get back I'll check with you tonight or tomorrow to see if we got the job."

"Okay. Keep your fingers crossed," she called as she backed out of the driveway.

Going from Lakewood to Applewood didn't take long. Alexandra was right on schedule when she turned onto the private road she'd been instructed to take. Evan Daniels's sprawling white-brick U-shaped home sat in the middle of lush grounds that were still July green. She pulled around the semicircular brick drive and parked in front of open wrought-iron gates.

As she locked her car doors she checked her reflection in the window. Then she headed for the house.

The courtyard floor within the U shape was marble and the click of Alexandra's heels as she crossed it echoed off the walls. Although the structure was ranch style she knew there would be cathedral ceilings inside just by the height of the double front doors. A uniformed maid answered the bell.

So far, so impressive, she thought as she went in.

"If you'll come this way I'll show you to the collection room where Mr. Daniels will join you," the maid said in modulated tones.

Alexandra followed the woman through a sunken living room carpeted in plush cream-colored wool. She couldn't tell anything about the furniture because it was still hidden under dustcovers, but she had no doubt it was the finest.

The collection room connected to the living room by tall double doors. Inside were several randomly placed pedestaled stands and display cases, a few wall shelves and a centrally positioned display table—all empty.

"These are pictures of the collection, if you'd care to look through them while you wait," the maid said, indicating a leather-covered album sitting on the display table.

At the sound of the doors closing after the maid, Alexandra took a look around the room in which her whole modest house would fit. She whistled softly in appreciation of the size alone. Then she took a notepad out of her purse and looked again, this time with more thought to her job.

There were two windows, wide and short, both of them high up on the walls. An experienced burglar could manage them without too much difficulty, probably getting to them from the roof; but a garden-variety crook would more than likely bypass them. And since they were out of easy reach, a touch-sensitive alarm could be used. Alexandra made note of what she would recommend.

She was glad to see that the only entrance was through the living room; a door that opened to the outside would present more of a complication.· The same cream-colored carpeting continued into the collection room, so a low-lying laser would be the first thing she'd suggest, with sensors in the floor only if a more elaborate system was what the client wanted.

Track lighting ran the perimeter of the room—a setup that would make a camera unobtrusive to the decor. Again Alexandra made notes although, without knowing what the collection consisted of or how valuable it was, she put a question mark beside it. The use of closed-circuit cameras in a private home was uncommon, but not unheard of.

Having taken care of the preliminaries, Alexandra turned to the album on the display table. It was obvious by all the oak cases and the shelves that took up wall space that the collection was not of paintings. She'd had experience with just about anything that could be collected: sculpture, rocks, coins, medieval weapons, clowns, dolls, guns; she'd even been asked to give a bid on a system to protect stuffed birds!

Alexandra opened the album cover to the first page. Clocks. She studied a color picture of a tall case clock with an intricate floral design carved around the face. The description under the picture explained that the pendulum and bob were solid gold. *Valuable* clocks.

On the second page were three German musical clocks followed by several nineteenth-century French ones, all in hand-carved casings, boxes or cabinets.

Then she turned the page again.

Watches, too. Antique watches.

So this wasn't simply a clock collection but a time-piece collection.

There were three pages of different American rail-road pocket watches pictured, only a few of them with fobs and chains attached. European pocket watches came next—beautiful faces hand-painted with flowers and leaves, or ships, or landscapes. There were watches with carvings of work scenes—farmers in a field, a butcher at a chopping block. The explanation for these outlined which parts of the carving were hinged or jointed to actually change position. There were skeleton watches that revealed the movements, and some whose cases were exquisitely carved or painted or jeweled. There were ring watches and buttonhole watches and antique pendant watches. There was a watch inside a gold skull-shaped case and even a vintage children's watch decorated with a primitive-looking Mickey Mouse.

And then, alone on a full page, there was a relatively plain but very delicate-looking pocket watch—simple bronze Roman numerals on a face years had colored cream. It had thin, unremarkable hands, a plain gold case.

But it made Alexandra catch her breath.

Incredulous, she leaned nearer and read the explanation beneath the picture. "Dated 1815 and signed by

Abraham-Louis Breguet. A quarter repeater—when the button on the stem is pulled out, turned and pushed back in, it chimes the hour and quarter hour.''

Abraham-Louis Breguet. The finest French watchmaker.

Alexandra knew because on the wall in her living room at home there was a picture of one of his watches hanging from the vest of her great-grandfather.

Except that this wasn't just another of Breguet's watches. It was the same watch. She knew, because there, on the case frame, were the notches: six of them, one over each of the first six Roman numerals. The sixth one was Tommy's.

Fate had an ironic sense of humor, Alexandra thought, to bring her here to give a bid on a security system to protect that watch.

Or *was* it just a coincidence?

"Of course it is," she said to herself. It had to be. And probably not even a very odd coincidence. The watch had been sold here in Colorado eight years ago as a collector's item. There couldn't be too many collectors who could afford a piece this expensive—and the alarm system to protect it. Since her company installed exclusive alarm systems, the odds of it crossing her path again were probably pretty good.

Just a coincidence.

"See something you like?"

Startled, Alexandra jumped. A steadying hand that could easily palm a basketball reached her arm instantly.

"I'm sorry. I didn't mean to scare you. I thought you heard me come in," the same deep, resonant voice said from beside her.

Alexandra put her hand over her racing heart and breathed a little laugh. "I didn't."

She looked up then—all the way up what had to be a full foot of height over her five feet three inches—to the man's face. Killer smile, she thought, catching sight of the slightly off-center tilt of his lips above a deep dimple in his chin. Then she widened her view to include his thin, very straight nose, square brow and eyes that were a darker blue than hers, more a midnight blue. He wasn't an image of male perfection, but there was a strength and a very masculine appeal in his face. With his carelessly swept-back waves of wheat-colored hair, he was definitely a man that any woman would take a second look at.

He rubbed her arm in a friendly, comforting gesture. "Are you okay?"

Alexandra took a deep breath to steady herself, managing to let her shoulders relax into a normal position. "I'm fine. Nothing like a little rush of adrenaline to keep me on my toes."

"Or to knock you on your keister."

It was the last thing Alexandra expected him to say, and she laughed just before glancing down at her feet and then back to him. "No, I'm still standing." She held her hand out. "I'm Alexandra Dunbar from Security Systems."

He let go of her arm and took her hand in a firm grip. "I'm Evan Daniels."

"Mr. Daniels."

"Please, call me Evan. The only one who's that formal around here is my housekeeper and I'm trying to break her of the habit."

"Evan, then." He was still holding her hand, staring into her face as if he'd forgotten that courtesy demanded he let go and move on. It struck Alexandra as odd how aware she was of the feel of his palm against hers, of the warmth generated there.

"Alexandra," he said again, as if he were trying it out. "Beautiful name. It sounds dignified and sort of old-world. I've never met an Alexandra before. I hope you're not called Alex for short. It's too masculine for you."

She assured him that she didn't use a nickname, feeling uncomfortable with the personal turn this meeting had taken. Especially when he still held her hand. Hoping to remind him of her purpose, she asked, "Was it your secretary I spoke to on the phone?"

Apparently it worked, because he finally let go of her. Slowly Alexandra pulled her hand back, closing it into a soft fist as if to capture the sensation. Then she realized he was talking and she wasn't listening.

"It was my assistant, Brian Levar, who called you. He'll be here shortly—I want his input. Meanwhile, would you like coffee or tea?"

"Nothing, thanks."

"Then, why don't we spend the time by you telling me a little about Security Systems."

He was a big man in more than just height. His shoulders were wide enough to block her view of most of the room, and his biceps stretched the sleeves of his white polo shirt and bulged even below the band. He was squarely built with only a slight V shape to his torso before charcoal-colored slacks formed a smooth line down long legs.

Alexandra realized that this time it was she who had momentarily forgotten this was business. "I started the company about a year ago. My grandfather taught me to be a locksmith when I was a teenager—'Everyone should have a trade,' he said. Then I went to college in Boulder and when I got out I just sort of drifted into the business side of locks and keys. I was with Blocker's Locksmiths and Alarms for ten years. Then I decided to try my own wings. Security Systems is fully bonded and I have references, if you'd care to see them," she offered in her best businesslike demeanor.

She wasn't sure what it was, but something made him smile. "I don't think I need to see references. My assistant had heard good things about the company, which is why I asked him to call you. Are you the sole owner?"

He asked the question in such a friendly way it almost seemed as if he were just interested rather than interviewing her. That was why this didn't really feel like a business meeting, she decided when she again needed to remind herself that it was.

"Security Systems is one hundred percent my baby."

"What? You didn't even let your husband or your 'significant other' in on it?" he teased.

"I don't have a husband or a 'significant other,' but even if I did I would have done this on my own. It was my goal to be my own boss."

He smiled again—a slow, Cheshire-cat kind of smile. Standing with her in front of the display table, he shifted his weight to one hip and crossed his arms over his expansive chest. Alexandra noticed that he wore a very expensive, dime-thin black watch and that there was no wedding ring on his left hand. Not that it mattered.

"Is business good?" he asked.

"As good as I expected it to be in the first year. But it's getting better all the time," she was quick to add, conscious of the company's image.

"The first year in any business is tough. But I admire the courage to give it a try. Especially on your own and as a woman. Many people talk about it, but when it comes to taking the risk it's a whole different story."

She was flattered, but it was the kind of compliment that didn't exactly call for gratitude so instead she said, "It's risky, all right."

"Are you a native of Colorado?" he asked, keeping her enveloped in that navy blue gaze of his.

"No, but I've been in Denver since college."

He finally took his eyes off her to glance around the room full of disarrayed furniture. "I'm not quite as new to Colorado as I look. I was raised here, wandered away after college and now I'm back to stay."

So she'd read. The business section of the *Rocky Mountain News* had run a piece highlighting his return. Local boy made good had been the angle, going on to explain that he'd hit the big time with his own investment company. The article had portrayed him as an intelligent, astute businessman whose return to Denver was a good sign for the future of local economy.

Alexandra had come away from reading the article with an altogether different impression of Evan Daniels than she was getting now. Nowhere had it been written that he had a warm, casual, unpretentious manner, that he was personable, down-to-earth, easy to talk to or just plain nice. And without a picture, there had been no way of knowing how attractive he was.

Annoyed that her thoughts were again straying, she forced her attention to the matter at hand. "You've picked a good room for your collection—in terms of security. High windows and no outside entrance are big plusses."

"I don't know if Brian told you—there's a general alarm system throughout the place. The previous owners had it installed. But we both thought the collection should have something more sophisticated."

"Your assistant did tell me about the other system. As I told him, I've worked with it before. It's a good one, particularly since it feeds in directly to the police. But you're right to have something more sensitive put in for such a valuable collection." She nodded in the direction of the album.

Evan Daniels's eyebrows arched charmingly, showing his enthusiasm. "Are you familiar with antique clocks and watches?"

"No," she answered too quickly. "I just assumed from what I saw of the pictures—what with the ages of some of the pieces and so forth.... Well, they're so beautiful they must be very valuable."

"They are something, aren't they?" he said.

"Yes," she agreed.

"The artistry that goes into them—the clockwork and the cases, all of it—fascinates me." He turned a different sort of smile on her—one that reminded her of Tommy's roguishness. "Is there artistry in burglar alarms? It doesn't seem as if there is in what I do."

"Artistic burglar alarms? I don't know about that. But I can guarantee that everything will be either completely out of sight or at least as unobtrusive as possible."

He smiled as if she'd amused him again. "Do you put them in yourself? Are you going to show up in overalls and a tool belt next time I see you? Or do you let someone else do that, at least?"

"The dirty work, you mean? I have an installation crew of three men. And, unless something unforeseeable happens, when we begin a job we stay with it until it's completely finished. There aren't any stops and starts."

"You know," he remarked, barely managing to keep his smile from turning into a full-fledged grin, "if your business doesn't make it, you definitely have a future in sales."

She had been giving the hard sell, hadn't she? But she was sensing something sort of electric in the air between them, and business was her ground wire. Still, not wanting to appear unfriendly, she smiled and vowed silently to tone it down. "Car dealers are after me all the time," she joked.

"I don't doubt it for a minute. But does it ever occur to them to put you to work?"

Again his humor caught her off guard. "I walked right into that one, didn't I?" she said and laughed.

"I don't mean to give you a hard time. But you seem so tense, I just wanted to loosen things up if I could." He uncrossed his arms and took a step away from her. "Maybe if I get something in here to sit on it'll help."

He was back again within minutes carrying three barstools. "Grab this one under my arm before I drop it, will you?"

Alexandra obliged him, then climbed up onto a stool, catching the clean, sea scent of his after-shave as she did.

Only after he saw that she was settled did he sit on the stool to her right, swivelling it toward her and hooking the heels of his loafers on the bottom rung, bringing muscular thighs very near.

"There, that's better. Are you sure you wouldn't like something to drink?"

"Positive," she said. This time it was Alexandra who couldn't suppress a grin. "You know I'm supposed to be here selling you a burglar alarm."

"Does that mean you can't relax and be comfortable?"

"No. It just means you don't have to treat me like an honored guest."

He winked at her. "My mother taught me to treat everyone that way."

His eyes locked with hers for a moment before the sound of another man's voice interrupted. "Sorry I held this up."

Was Evan Daniels a little slow in turning his gaze from her or was she just imagining it?

"That's all right," Evan assured. "Alexandra Dunbar, this is my assistant and longtime friend, Brian Levar, the man you spoke to on the phone. Brian, Alexandra Dunbar, owner, proprietor and crackerjack saleswoman of Security Systems."

Again Alexandra offered her hand as the other man joined them. Tall and blond, with striking green eyes, Brian Levar had features that could only be called "chiseled." Had he the inclination, Alexandra had no doubt he could have been a male model. And yet, more than anything, she appreciated his presence, feeling sure that a third party would put this meeting back on a business course—a course from which it seemed to have veered.

"Well, shall we get to work?" She didn't wait for a response before putting her briefcase on the display table and opening it.

Brian sat on the stool to her left. As Alexandra took out her brochures she felt more than saw Evan's arm go across the back of her stool. He leaned toward her for a better glimpse of the pamphlets and she again caught a whiff of his intoxicating after-shave. But she needed a clear head, so she set some of the leaflets on top of the leather-bound album near him. As she did, she thought again of the Breguet watch.

"Do you mind if I ask how you heard about Security Systems?" she asked Brian.

"I saw an interview you did on a local show not long ago. When we started talking about a new alarm for the collection room I remembered you. Evan is big on helping new businesses."

The interview. One of the factors that increased the likelihood of this being a coincidence. She relaxed a little.

With her materials finally set up, Alexandra went into her presentation. "The first thing I'd like to do is seal those windows permanently," she began.

Outlining what she had decided was the best combination for protection, Alexandra addressed both men equally. As she did, she felt an unaccountably heightened awareness of Evan's presence.

"Well, here are the damages," she said when she finished her calculations, handing her notepad to Evan.

He looked over her figures, nodding his head as he did. Then he sat back. "Okay. When can you start?"

Easy as that and she had the job. Elation, or at least relief, should have been what Alexandra felt. But instead it was a sudden surge of uneasiness that went through her. Why? she wondered.

Was it because of Tommy and the watch?

But did her grandfather even know who owned the Breguet now? Did he care anymore?

Surely if he knew or if he cared he would have said something. But he hadn't. And if she kept quiet about this coincidence, the chances were the watch would stay out of his thoughts.

Still, the uneasiness persisted and it was too strong to ignore.

"Are you sure you wouldn't like to have a couple of other bids to compare with before you decide?" she asked, almost hoping for a legitimate way out of this too-good-to-be-true job offer.

"I don't need any other bids. I want you to do the job," Evan answered in that deep voice that smoothed over her like warm honey. He gave her back the notepad, and as he did his hand brushed hers, making her aware once more of the odd sensitivity she had to him.

It wasn't Tommy and the watch that gave her this disquiet, Alexandra realized. It was Evan Daniels and her own reaction to him. And that realization relieved some of the uneasiness. Being overly aware of a man was controllable.

This was a job like any other and it had come at a time when she really needed the work. Nothing else mattered.

"We can be here Monday morning, bright and early, if that's all right with you."

Alexandra was glad to see John's truck still parked in front of her house when she pulled into the driveway. She'd gone to the bank on her way home to deposit Evan's down payment for half of the agreed-upon price for the security system, and now she could write John a check for all he had coming in back wages. Taking the job had been a good idea, she decided, in spite of some faintly lingering doubts.

"Where's Tommy?" she asked when she had come through the empty house to find John at the desk in her office.

"He went to the grocery store. You didn't have the right kind of cheese for tacos."

Alexandra kicked off her shoes. "I'll bet he talked your ear off the whole time I was gone and you're still here because this is the first chance you've had to get anything done."

"On the nose," John confirmed with a laugh.

"Well, I'm glad, because I can actually make good on what I owe you."

"We got the job?" he guessed.

"With half the money up front. It's already in the bank, so you can cash your check on the way home."

"Don't pay me if there's something else you need the money for, Alexandra. It's okay. I know you're good for it."

"Thanks, John. I don't know what I'd do without you. But catching up on your salary is the reason I wanted this job so badly."

John closed the file he'd been looking through and got up so that she could get to the checkbook in the desk drawer. "When do we start?"

"Monday morning. The house is off 36th and Youngsfield. In fact—" she stopped writing the check and handed him her estimate tablet from her briefcase "—here's a list of what I sold. You can order everything we need while I do this, so it'll be ready and waiting Monday morning.''

When John hung up the phone he said, ''All set. Everything's in stock. If you give me the address I'll pick up the materials and go straight to the job on Monday. By the way, what are we doing for Mr. Evan Daniels?''

''Wiring a display room for his collection.''

''What's he collect?''

John was going to find out sooner or later. It might as well be now. ''Timepieces.''

He took the check she held out for him. ''As in watches?'' he asked with a slight frown.

Alexandra nodded. Should she tell him about the Breguet? There wasn't any reason for him to know. ''Watches and clocks,'' she confirmed.

''No kidding.'' He chuckled. ''After all that went down over Tommy's old watch, here you are being paid to put in an alarm to protect the same kind of thing. That's really weird, isn't it?''

If you only knew. ''Isn't it, though.'' After another moment's hesitation she said, ''Uh, I'd rather not let Tommy know that's what the collection is, okay? There's no reason to stir things up.''

John folded his check and put it in his wallet. ''He won't hear it from me.''

''Does Tommy ever mention the old watch to you?'' she asked cautiously.

''Sometimes.''

''That's funny. He never talks about it to me. I was hoping he'd forgotten about it.''

''Not likely.''

''What did he say?''

John shrugged. "Nothing much. Mostly that I have to be careful of women so one doesn't do to me what Marjorie did to him, and how sorry he is that a woman cost him the watch."

Alexandra nodded. She'd heard Tommy say that before. "I wonder if he knows who owns it now. Has he said?"

John folded the paper on which Alex had written Evan's name and address and put it in his shirt pocket. "Not to me. Why?"

"No reason. Talking about watches today just made me think about it."

"Seems like it's more on your mind than on Tommy's."

She hoped he was right about that.

"Well, unless you want me to stick around I think I'll take off," John said. "You'll be at the job when I get there Monday morning?"

"Absolutely."

"See you then."

Alex watched her old friend leave, but it wasn't John she was thinking about; it was Evan Daniels.

Where did that come from? she wondered.

And while she was at it, she wondered why all of a sudden the weekend that stretched out before her seemed endless.

Chapter Two

"Congratulate me, I'm an uncle!" Evan said into the telephone when the hospital's switchboard had connected him to his sister early Monday morning.

"You have it wrong," Jeannie answered with a laugh. "You're supposed to congratulate me for being a new mom."

"Is that how it works?" he teased. "Well then, congratulations, *Mom*! Is everything okay?"

"Everything is great. Your new niece is five pounds, three ounces of beautiful pink pucker with the sweetest little face you've ever seen and six absolutely gorgeous hairs."

"You counted her hairs?"

His sister laughed. "I counted everything."

"How about you? Have you done laps around the maternity floor yet?"

"Not quite, but I feel pretty good. Sturdy stock, you know. We'll go home tomorrow."

"Which brings us to the gift I've decided to give you."

"It'd better be good if you want to be godfather."

"It's Mary and Stan."

"You're giving your first niece two human beings as a birth gift? I don't think you can do that anymore, Evan."

"I'm giving you their services."

"I know Mary is your housekeeper, but who is Stan?"

"Her husband. He lost his job a few months ago and hasn't been able to get another one. Things have been tough for them so I hired him for odd jobs. Mary can cook and clean and help with the baby, and Stan can get the nursery painted and the furniture set up—unless you were thinking of making my niece sleep in a dresser drawer."

"No, we were thinking of putting her in a box beside the bed with a hot-water bottle and a clock. After all, it worked for the puppy."

"Treat that baby right or I'll take her."

"Sorry, big brother, that's the easy way. You're going to have to go out and make one of your own."

"And making one of my own is easier said than done without a partner."

"It's getting a partner that's easier said than done," Jeannie amended.

"Or getting an honest one, anyway," Evan added wryly.

"I can't believe I set you up with a married woman. I'm so sorry."

"Relax, Jeannie. You apologized eight times last night, remember? You had no way of knowing Shelline was married—she lied to everyone."

Jeannie's tone became more serious. "I really thought she was the girl for you."

"It just wasn't meant to be, I guess. Sooner or later one of us is bound to come up with somebody who'll help me give your new daughter cousins. In the meantime, what do we do about the housewarming?"

"I'm still throwing it—it isn't until the end of next week. Most everything is already done, and with Mary and her husband helping out I don't think there'll be any problem. Unless you don't think you can have the house in shape without their help."

"All that's left here is some furniture arranging and picture hanging. Even the security system should be in before that, so I can have the collection room set up."

"Great. Oh, I have to go. The nurse just brought the baby. Talk to you later."

Evan hung up. Mention of the burglar alarm brought with it thoughts of Alexandra Dunbar. She'd been on his mind a lot over the weekend.

He really liked the lady.

She'd struck him as unique from the first moment he'd set eyes on her. Just the way she looked was a novelty—waist-length strawberry-ice-colored hair, pale, pale eyes, high cheekbones, that thin nose, those soft-looking lips.

And he'd loved her laugh. Her whole face had lit up and her eyes had glistened like blue diamonds. He could make a fool of himself just trying to get to see and hear it again.

She seemed quick, bright, sharp; he knew she was beautiful, and, unless he was mistaken, there had been some kind of click between them.

He was intrigued, all right. In fact he'd spent the whole weekend looking forward to this morning when he would see her again. This time he wasn't going to let her get away without—

"If you don't answer me pretty soon, Evan, I'm going to call the paramedics to come and revive you."

Evan shook his head slightly. "How long have you been standing there?" he asked Brian who was at the sideboard pouring himself a cup of coffee.

"Standing here? I've been doing more than standing here. I've been talking to you for the past five minutes while you stared into space with that strange smile on your face."

"Guess I was lost in thought."

"Guess so. I came in here and told you your shares in Northridge Gas and Electric just sold for six times what you paid and you didn't even hear me."

"Six times, huh?"

"Too late to cover up, Evan. I've known you too long. I'll bet you haven't thought about anything but our lovely burglar-alarm lady this whole weekend. I *know* she's all you've talked about."

"I can do things like that. You're the one getting married next month, not me."

"And you're jealous."

Evan conceded with a shrug. Sometimes it seemed as if everyone in the whole damn world were part of a couple. How could he be so lucky in business and investments and so unlucky in love?

Brian took a sip of his coffee. "So, you're interested in our burglar-alarm lady."

Evan looked thoughtful. "Could be."

"Well, good luck. I'll keep my fingers crossed that she doesn't lie or cheat, that she isn't one of the walking wounded or one of the man-haters, that she's healthy, not a gold digger, genuinely unmarried and uninvolved, and generally doesn't have any other skeletons in her closet."

Evan laughed. "Thanks."

"In the meantime I just wanted to bring you down to earth so we can get a little work done before the lady in question arrives and puts you back in your trance."

Alexandra turned away from her closet to look at the clock on her night table. She'd been standing there for twenty minutes trying to decide what to wear today. The last time it had taken her that long to choose an outfit she had been seventeen and suffering from a mad crush on John's cousin.

"Now that's a telling association," she muttered to herself, grabbing the next thing that caught her eye.

Going to Evan Daniels's house again this morning was nothing more than a courtesy she liked to offer her customers. She planned to arrive before the crew to introduce everyone rather than having John and his men go in cold.

But what she wore to do it usually wasn't such a big deal.

Who was she kidding? It had *never* been a big deal. Until this morning.

Her tan twill slacks had seemed too casual, the crepe pantsuit too dressy, the black slacks too worn around the hems and the navy pants and vest too much like the pinstriped suit she'd worn on Friday.

And what difference should it make if what she wore today was a lot like what she'd worn on Friday, for crying out loud?

"Okay. So I admit it," she muttered to herself.

Hadn't she spent the whole weekend thinking about her newest client? Hadn't she found herself looking forward to seeing him again this morning? Hadn't she gone over and over everything he'd said? How he'd looked? How his voice had sounded? And it wasn't just because Tommy had gone to the mountains for the weekend and she'd been alone—although that's what she'd told herself the whole time.

No. This was just like the crush she'd had at seventeen. Except that now she was considerably older than seventeen.

She buttoned her white blouse all the way to her throat, turned up the collar and pinned a small gold brooch over the top button. Then she slipped on a tapestry vest, cocoa-colored slacks and a matching blazer.

Still, it was kind of exciting to feel like this again, she decided. So what if she had a schoolgirl crush? What harm did it do? she asked herself as she brushed her hair and caught it back in a loose knot at her nape.

There was nothing wrong with admiration from afar, she reasoned. And after all, it had been a long time since she'd felt the anticipation of seeing the object of that crush again, wondering if he was really as attractive, as nice, as funny, as she had originally thought; fantasizing that he was as anxious to see her as she was to see him. It was a nice feeling, for a change. As long as she didn't do anything about it or even let anyone know, it was harmless—a little harmless admiration from afar. She decided to indulge in it and enjoy.

"I'm home," Tommy called just before a slam of the front door confirmed it.

Slipping her feet into brown pumps, Alexandra opened her bedroom door. "I'm sure glad. Somebody's tried calling you three times already this morning. Did you have a good weekend?"

Tommy stepped into the hallway. "Most of the aspens were already bare but it was beautiful anyway. You should have come with us, darling."

Alexandra refrained from saying that as much as she loved her grandfather, the thought of spending the weekend with a group of octogenarians from the Bingo Hut hadn't appealed to her. Instead she said, "I'm glad you had a good time."

"So who called?"

"I don't know. She wouldn't say or leave any message."

"*She?*"

"She. Someone you met at the senior center, maybe?"

He winked at her. "Could be one of a dozen. I've been handing out your card all over the place—you never know how many elderly ladies might be interested in a burglar alarm."

"I think this one must be interested in you. She didn't say anything about a burglar alarm." Alexandra took her purse off the doorknob and slipped it over her shoulder. "I'm sorry to rush off the moment you get in, but I have to get to this new client's house before John." Just then the phone rang and she rolled her eyes. "That's probably your girlfriend again. You answer the phone and I'll get out of here. See you later."

"You look pretty spiffy today," he called after her.

Alexandra waved and said thanks over her shoulder just before she closed the door.

After she parked outside the open gates to Evan's home Alexandra crossed the courtyard as quickly as if she were late. The housekeeper, Mary, answered her knock. "I'll let him know you're here," she told Alexandra, leaving her in the living room this time. When Mary came back only minutes later, she said, "Mr. Daniels asked if you would join him at the stables. When your workmen arrive I'll call you both."

The stables? "Okay," Alexandra agreed.

Mary led her through a huge kitchen dominated by an enormous butcher's block in the center and furnished with rich wood cupboards and oversize state-of-the-art appliances that any chef would have been thrilled to use. On the far side, French doors opened onto a brick path.

"The walkway leads directly to the stables," Mary informed her, leaving Alexandra to go on alone.

The path ran parallel to a brick wall, on the other side of which was a meticulously trimmed hedge. Peeking over it Alexandra caught a glimpse of an oval-shaped swimming pool—covered for the winter—and a small cottage on the opposite side, with enough distance from the main house to allow both places privacy but not so far from either the main house or the pool to seem completely isolated.

"This is some place," Alexandra said to herself as the walkway veered from the tiled pool and patio and the manicured hedges and gardens that surrounded it all. What came into view then was another small, less elaborate building, whitewashed to look almost fluorescent in the October sunshine. Since it adjoined a white-rail fenced paddock, she assumed it was the stable and not another cottage, as it well could have been.

"You're early. You said you'd be here just shortly before your men, so I thought I had a while yet," Evan called to her from the doorway at the end of the path.

She took in the full image of him from bottom to top. He looked wonderful. Tan boots poked out from beneath jeans that hugged his muscular thighs and slim hips like an ardent lover. His honey-colored chamois-cloth shirt stretched taut across the breadth of his shoulders, and its sleeves were rolled nearly to his elbows. His face looked morning fresh and clean-shaven, his hair combed and left to fall slightly into the wave she'd bet he had trouble taming. Alexandra decided that, all in all, he was food for fantasy for years to come.

Then she remembered his comment about her being early and glanced at her watch. This morning, in her anxiousness to see Evan again, she hadn't realized just how early she was. John wasn't due for a good half-hour.

"I guess I am. I didn't realize," she explained as she reached him. "I can wait in the house if you're busy," she offered, hoping he wouldn't take her up on it.

He shook his head, those dark blue eyes of his straying on her as one corner of his mouth quirked up in a smile. "No, come on in—unless you hate horses. I always like to show off my beasts."

"I love horses. I'd like to see them."

Evan stepped out onto the path and waited for her to precede him. Alexandra breathed in the earthy scent of horses, oats and hay which brought with it an instant, vivid memory from her childhood.

There were six stalls but only two of them were occupied. "This guy is Cotter." Evan introduced the first horse, a sable-colored stallion. He patted the animal's rump and moved to the next. "And over here we have his family—Livvy, who's a peach of a horse, and her foal. I've been calling him Sal."

Livvy was a red mare and Sal looked like a miniature version. Alexandra stroked the mare's nose and made friends before turning her attention to the irresistible colt. "Sal?" she repeated with a laugh. "You make him sound like a gangster."

"I beg your pardon. Sal is the name of my favorite uncle and he was not a gangster," Evan said. But he was smiling, so she knew he hadn't taken offense. "What would *you* call him? Blaze, or Star for the white patch on his nose? Lightning? Thunder? Tom?"

Alexandra laughed. "Not Tom. My grandfather wouldn't appreciate having a horse named after him." The colt nuzzled her hand when she tried to take it away. "Maybe I'd call him Sugar because he's that sweet."

"Sugar? You'd call what will be a strapping stallion Sugar? He'd be laughed right out of the pasture. All the other horses would make fun of him and no mare would so much as flip her tail at him. It would be devastating for him," he teased with dramatic exaggeration.

"So instead, he's Sal the Strapping Stallion," she goaded him.

"Absolutely. Then he'll be able to hold his head up with the best of them."

Alexandra watched Evan reach around and smooth the side of Sal's neck. She could suddenly feel that same hand on her arm as it had been on Friday. A pleasant little shiver ran up her spine. She took in the sight of his strong wrist, speckled with wheat-colored hairs and wrapped in that thin black watch. Ah, yes, there was lots of food for future fantasies.

"Well, no matter what his name is, he's beautiful," she said to fill in the silence that her appreciation of her client had left. "How old is he?"

"He's not quite a month yet. But the barn is heated, so he'll be fine through the winter."

Alexandra took a handful of grain out of a nearby bucket and fed it to Livvy from her palm.

"Do you ride?" Evan asked, leaning on an elbow he propped along the top of the stall wall and shifting his weight to one hip as he rested the instep of his boot on the bottom board.

"I used to in the old days," she answered before she realized she was using one of Tommy's terms.

"The 'old' days?"

"When I was a kid," she amended.

"Did you have a horse of your own?"

"Sort of. She wasn't a thoroughbred like these. But she could dance."

He chuckled with a rich sound that rumbled from his chest. "She could dance?" he repeated in disbelief.

"And roll over and play dead like a dog. She was very talented."

"It would seem. What happened to her?"

"Oh, times changed and we had to let her go," she said vaguely.

"Did it break your heart?"

"A little," she admitted, smiling at him. "Did you have horses as a kid?"

"No, but I paid to ride whenever I could and made it one of my goals to buy one of my own as soon as money allowed."

"Is Sal the beginning of becoming a breeder?"

"No, he's the product of Cotter and Livvy's overwhelming attraction for each other."

"Oh. Well." In her present state of mind his comment had struck too close to home. "Do you plan to become a horse breeder?" she asked, hoping it was a quick enough recovery to hide her reaction. But when she glanced at him, she found him grinning and sensed he'd seen through her.

"Breeding horses as a business doesn't interest me, no. Sal was just an accidental dividend."

Alexandra was grateful that he didn't tease her about her embarrassment. "Are you planning to race them?" she asked then.

He shook his head. "I don't look at everything as a moneymaking proposition. The horses are strictly for my own pleasure. Just a hobby."

Alexandra was fresh out of horse questions and so moved back to the first stall and stroked Cotter's nose. "We've been neglecting you over here, haven't we, Dad?" she said to the animal.

Evan followed her, handing her the grain pail from the other stall. "You can't hand-feed this guy. He was abused before I got him. But you can pretty safely feed him from the bucket if you want."

Alexandra accepted the pail and held it for the horse, talking soothingly to him as he ate.

"I wouldn't have figured you for a woman who likes horses," Evan mused a moment later.

"Why is that?"

"Oh, I don't know. You struck me as the quintessential modern career woman. The last thing I pictured you doing was mucking around with horses."

She glanced around the spotless stable. "This is hardly mucking around."

"You still strike me as an interesting combination of contradictions. I like it."

What could she say to that? "I think we've hit bottom" was what she settled on, referring to the empty grain bucket.

"Cotter's a chow hound. He'll always eat as much as there is. It probably comes from the abuse. I guess even horses who starve end up feeling like they'd better take as much as they can get when they can get it."

"Someone starved a thoroughbred horse?"

"Sometimes there's no figuring people, is there? I called Animal Control and reported it but even that didn't have an effect. Apparently the owners came up with a plausible excuse. But poor old Cotter just kept getting thinner and thinner. I ended up taking the owner to court and buying the horse when the judgment finally took him away from them."

Spending time with this man, Alexandra realized, was a little dangerous. Her experience with fantasies was that the inspiration for them was never as good in reality. And yet this man only seemed to get better the more she got to know him.

"Not many people would go through all of that," she said, thinking, *especially not someone who could afford to go out and buy the best for themselves.* "The abuse might have been reported, but after that... Well, not many people would follow it through and end up providing the animal with a home themselves. I'm impressed."

Now it was Evan who didn't seem to know what to say to her compliment. He smoothed Cotter's mane. "I'd like it if you'd come riding with me sometime. Soon."

That took her off guard. "Oh, I couldn't."

"Why couldn't you?"

What was she supposed to say to that? That he'd been relegated to strictly fantasy status? She said the first thing she could think of: "I wouldn't want to be an imposition."

"That's hardly what you'd be. I'd love the company."

"Well, then, maybe sometime," she agreed vaguely, having no intention of following through with it.

"Good," he replied in a way that seemed to indicate he wasn't going to let her off the hook.

Just then the phone on the wall near the door rang. Alexandra looked at her watch. "That must be John and the guys."

"More than likely." Evan answered the phone on the second ring and within moments they were on the path leading back to the house.

"So what happens after you introduce me to your men?" he asked as they walked.

"I leave them to work and make the other calls I have today."

"Are you sure you shouldn't stay and oversee things?"

Did he mean that for personal reasons he would like her to? Or that he didn't trust her people? Alex opted for the latter. "My guys are completely trustworthy. I have full confidence in them. I'd only be in their way."

He held the back door open for her. "I don't doubt their abilities or their trustworthiness," he said as she passed in front of him.

So it had been for personal reasons.

Before Alexandra could think of anything to say to that, he held his arm out toward a doorway that connected the kitchen to a laundry room. "I'm going to make a pit stop to wash my hands. Join me?"

He could make even that sound enticing. "Definitely," she replied. "I like horses, but smelling like one for the rest of the day doesn't appeal to me."

The laundry room was clean, bright and efficient looking. Evan turned on the water in the washtub and held out a bottle of liquid soap. "Ladies first."

Alexandra pumped some into one palm and then made quick work of it. When she was finished, Evan handed her a clean towel from an overhead cupboard. While she dried her hands he took her place in front of the sink.

It was strange to find herself so drawn to the simple sight of a man washing up. But drawn she was. Those big hands worked the soap into a frothy lather, slip-sliding over and around each other. One after the other he squeezed a fist up each thumb and Alex felt a desire to have those hands on her, squeezing more than her thumbs. Then he worked the lather up his wrists in a rapid scrubbing motion that somehow translated itself to Alexandra as a wet, warm caress that her body suddenly seemed to crave.

He plunged his arms up to his elbows in the running water. The soap suds sluiced away and Alexandra had a flashing image of how his whole naked body might look being rinsed in a shower.

This fantasy was getting out of control. She took a deep breath and held it, forcing herself to look away. Her gaze caught on the watch he must have taken off while she'd washed her hands.

Then he turned to face her. "Can I share your towel?" he asked, nodding to the cloth she still held poised between her hands.

"Sure. Here." She gave it to him wondering if she'd lapsed into temporary insanity. And yet she still couldn't tear her eyes away as he dried his hands and then put his watch back on his wrist.

"All set," he said, apparently unaware of what was going on in her head, for which Alexandra was extremely grateful.

Twice on the way from the kitchen to the collection room he held a door open for her and in order to pass through, she had to come close enough to feel the heat of his body. She was glad to see familiar faces when they made it to where John was already giving instructions for beginning the job.

She introduced everyone and stood aside while Evan shook hands with all three workmen.

"Are you feeling okay?" John asked her when the amenities were over. "You look flushed."

"Do I?" Alexandra asked more brightly than she needed to. "I don't know why. I'm fine."

Her friend seemed to accept that as he turned to start work, and Alexandra decided it was time to bail out.

"Well, I'd better get going. John, you know where to reach me if you need me," she said. Then she turned to Evan with every intention of saying a fast goodbye and making an even faster exit.

But before she could say anything, he announced, "I'll walk you out."

How much easier everything would be if he didn't have such impeccable manners, she thought, heading for the front door. Again he reached around her to open it, following her all the way to her car.

"Have dinner with me tonight, Alexandra," he said as she reached for her car door handle.

"I'd like that," she heard herself answer, appalled that her mouth had been quicker than her brain.

"Great. Brian told me you worked out of your house, so I'll get your address off your card and pick you up at seven-thirty if that's all right."

It wasn't all right. Nothing about this was all right. He was supposed to be a fantasy. Only a fantasy. But since some impulse had already made her agree to the date, there wasn't anything she could do to change the situation. "Just name a restaurant and I'll meet you there," she suggested.

"Not a chance," Evan insisted forcefully. "When I take a woman to dinner I pick her up. Besides, it would be silly to take two cars when—if memory serves—you don't live all that far from here. I'll be there at half past seven."

What could she say? That just in case Tommy did know that Evan owned the Breguet watch, the last thing in the world she wanted was to introduce the two of them when she'd been so careful to keep this new client's name to herself?

Of course, she couldn't say that. And in her present condition she couldn't think of anything else to say, either. Instead she forced a smile. "I'll be ready," she managed weakly, at the same time trying to figure a way to get Tommy out of the house by seven.

Chapter Three

It was late that afternoon when Evan saw Brian's car coming down the drive. He'd finished his paperwork for the day, so he headed through the kitchen, poaching a dozen of Mary's still-warm oatmeal cookies from a cooling rack on the way.

With cookie plate in hand, he paused outside to smell the October-crisp air. Then he rounded the pool and knocked on the door of the guest cottage, the living space Brian would shortly vacate to share his future wife's larger place.

Rather than seeing the door open, though, Evan heard the bedroom window at the corner of the house slide up. He stepped back slightly to see Brian, with the phone receiver cradled against his shoulder, motioning him to come in.

Evan let himself in and set the cookies on the coffee table before going into the tiny kitchen. He took two glasses from a cupboard and then made a stop at the refrigerator for milk, bringing everything into the living room.

Brian had shucked his tie and suit coat and left them over the back of the brown plaid sofa. Evan moved them to a barstool and sat at one end of the couch to wait for his friend. Relaxing back, he became aware for the first time that in the silence of the small house Brian's voice carried through the adjoining door, which was slightly ajar. Not wanting to eavesdrop, Evan stood, closed the door and headed for the corner where he had helped Brian set up his friend's elaborate stereo system when they'd moved in to this compound.

But the corner was empty.

Evan stopped short and glanced around the room. That stereo was Brian's baby. Where was it?

Nowhere Evan could see. And if it wasn't in the living room, where could it be? Ten thousand dollars' worth of audio equipment wouldn't fit in the small bedroom along with the bed, dressers and TV that Evan had furnished it with. Perhaps Brian had moved it to Karla's; that seemed a likely enough explanation.

Evan sat back down, hoping Brian's conversation wouldn't be so audible through the closed door. No such luck. He tried not to listen but it was virtually impossible, since he could hear almost every word Brian said. Then he realized his childhood friend was exploring the possibility of selling a very valuable stock, and concern made him forget courtesy to listen in earnest.

When Brian came out a few moments later, Evan couldn't help himself from commenting. "I didn't mean to overhear, but there wasn't any way to avoid it.

You can't really be thinking about selling that RTM stock?''

Brian shrugged and sat on the other side of the sofa. ''Yes, I can be.''

''Don't do it. You know it's low at the moment because of their change in command and that it'll skyrocket once the new CEO gets in the driver's seat.''

''I also know that it's the biggest block of stock I have and the only one I can liquidate at the moment.''

''You need money?''

''It's not your problem, Evan,'' Brian said, taking a cookie and his milk with him as he leaned back and put his feet on the coffee table.

''Where's your stereo?'' Evan asked when it occurred to him where it might have gone.

''I sold it.''

Evan was getting the picture. Whatever was going on was pretty desperate. ''And now you're thinking about selling the RTM stock. Your shares have to be worth about ten thousand at the moment. In two months they'll be at fifty, maybe sixty thousand. The last thing you want to do is sell.''

''True.''

''Then why are you?''

Brian dropped his head onto the sofa back and pinched the bridge of his nose in seeming fatigue. ''You know that restaurant franchise I went into partnership on with my brother?''

''In Philly? Yeah, I remember.''

''Well, it's failing. Without checking with me first, Bill has gotten the place in debt up to our eyeballs and if we don't find some big bucks soon, the whole deal is going under. That will mean more of a loss to me than selling this stock now.''

"So, I'll give you a loan."

Brian shook his head. "No. Thanks anyway."

Evan had heard that tone before. Brian's pride was an element in this. "I'll charge you an arm and a leg in interest if it would make you feel better," he offered. "But even that won't cost you what selling the RTM stock will. Hell, even after it goes back up it's likely to triple again in two years."

"Thanks, but no thanks." Brian jammed his hand through his hair. "I will sell the stock to you, though, if you want it."

"Keep it in your name and I'll hold it for collateral if it makes you feel better."

Brian looked over at him from beneath a frown. "I'm doing this on my own, Evan. It's my brother and my oversight that got us into this mess. It's going to be me that bails us out."

There was a finality in that statement that warned Evan the subject was closed. For a while neither of them said anything. Evan placed one ankle over the opposite knee and stared at his foot, wondering whether or not to get what was bothering him off his chest. In the end he decided that his friendship with Brian was too valuable to leave under the burden of silence. "You know, in the last few months I keep getting the feeling that I'm walking on eggs with you about some things that I thought were resolved. Is there something we could talk about and clear the air?"

Brian groaned. "It's not you," he said. "It's me."

Evan kept quiet, waiting.

"Getting married is a big step," Brian went on. "I wanted to go into it feeling like I could take care of everything, handle everything, provide everything. I thought I'd overcome those ego problems I had ten years ago—the ones that had me refusing to admit you knew more and had a better instinct about stocks and investments than I did, those same ego problems that ended up making me invest in the opposite of everything you did and losing my shirt at the same time you were flush enough to open your own company. Since I wised up and signed to work with you, I didn't think I minded hanging on to your coattails. But ever since I got engaged I've been feeling like I should be able to do it all myself." Brian breathed a wry laugh. "It's like I have to prove to Karla that I'm as good as you are when it comes to money."

"Well, hell, nobody's that good," Evan said, using an old joke between them to diffuse some of the tension in the room.

It worked, because Brian lifted his head off the back of the couch and sneered at him. "Money is the only thing you have up on me. And to prove it I'll take you out onto the tennis court and whip your rear end just for starters."

"Yeah? You and what army?"

"Just me and my racquet and one hand tied behind my back," Brian replied, volleying his return of the exchange they'd been having since they were kids. Then he got serious again. "Look, the point here is that I went out on a limb with the restaurant. I should have kept closer tabs on my brother. I should have had more of a hand in the business. It was my mistake, and right now it's important to me that I do whatever I have to do to take care of it. Call it macho or whatever you like, but it's a big thing to me to get the restaurant back on course and make a success of it without your help."

"And is selling the RTM stock going to do it?"

"Truthfully? I don't know. It may not be enough. But I'm doing it just the same."

"So you're going to sell the stock no matter what I say?"

"I'd buy it if I were you," Brian advised.

"I suppose I'd be asking to be knocked off my block to offer you over market value because I'm so sure it's going to go up."

"You suppose right."

"How about an option to buy it back?"

"That I'll take."

"Okay, then. Come on over to the house and I'll write you a check. Then I have a date to get ready for."

"Don't tell me. You're going out with our lady of the burglar alarm."

"The one and only. I'd ask you and Karla to go along, but frankly I want her all to myself." Evan stood and went to the door. But before he left he turned back to his friend. "Good luck with the restaurant."

"Thanks. Good luck with the woman."

"You look like you had a good day," Tommy greeted as Alexandra came in just before five that afternoon.

"Pretty good," she responded as she put her shopping bags on the camelback sofa in the living room. "How was yours?"

"Perfect," Tommy said with a flourish. "Absolutely perfect. One of the best days I've had since I got here."

Alexandra laughed at his enthusiasm. "What did you do to make it so absolutely perfect? Clean the refrigerator again? Or maybe the stove this time?"

''Both,'' he confirmed with supreme satisfaction. ''But that wasn't what made it perfect.''

Alexandra set up the ironing board and iron. ''What did? Let me guess—whoever that woman was who called this morning before you got home caught up with you later?''

That had to be it, because her grandfather's face erupted into a grin that turned his skin into a web of wrinkles. ''Could be, but I'm not talking. A man has to have a little mystery to him. Or-r-r...'' He drew the word out like a drum roll. ''It could also be a surprise for you.''

Tommy was famous for his surprises. And he never gave them away. ''Then I know better than to try and weasel it out of you. Nobody keeps secrets the way you do.''

''So you went shopping, I see,'' Tommy said, after watching Alexandra take a new dress out of a sack and begin to iron it.

''I shouldn't have, but I have a dinner date tonight, and... Well, two of this afternoon's appointments accepted my bids, so I figured I could splurge.''

''Wonderful! Congratulations!'' He picked up the receipt that also listed a new belt and boots to match. ''Let me buy your celebration clothes.''

Alexandra grabbed her charge slip out of his hands. ''Not a chance.''

They'd had this kind of exchange at least once a day since he'd come to live with her and she'd never considered giving in to her grandfather. She didn't know exactly how much money Tommy had. She knew that eight years ago he had sold literally everything he owned, but she didn't have any idea what was left of that now, and she didn't care.

"I want you to keep whatever money you have for yourself," she told him without looking up from her ironing. "I'll take care of the everyday things." The same way Tommy had taken care of her after her parents had been killed. He'd raised her, paid her way through college, always been more generous with her than he should have been. Now it was her turn, and nothing was going to stop her from doing the same for him.

"Think about this, darling. After all, I'm only eighty-two," he said very seriously.

Alexandra tried to suppress a smile as she rearranged the dress on the ironing board to expose new wrinkles. "I know how old you are, Tommy."

"You also know that my father lived to be a hundred and three. That's another twenty-one years I could be around."

"Oh, I hope so," she answered earnestly. "And that's all the more reason I want to take care of the everyday expenses. As I recall, your father was still going to Las Vegas to gamble at ninety-nine. I want you to be able to, too, if the whim strikes."

"I have my social-security retirement benefits back now," Tommy said, as if reading her mind and reminding her that the cash he had was not his only money.

"We both know that barely keeps you in bingo and those awful foreign cigars you smoke."

"Only one a day," he defended indignantly. "And they're my single vice—albeit an expensive one since I can only get them on the black market."

Finished ironing her dress, Alexandra took it to her bedroom, laid it carefully on her bed and came back to put away the board. "I certainly don't want you to have to give up your single vice—even if they do smell like the inside of a Turkish prison."

"How would you know what the inside of a Turkish prison smells like?"

"Just a guess."

"Will you make me a promise, then?" Tommy asked, back to being serious again.

"You know I will."

"If you ever get strapped for money I'll be the first to know?"

Had she been the first to know when he was strapped for money? Hardly. She'd been the last. In fact, she hadn't even known about all those years of problems until long after they were over. Instead he'd protected her. "Would I ever not come to you with my problems?" she said rather than give the promise he'd asked for. Then, to distract him, she waved an irresistible carrot in front of his nose. "I think one of those boots I bought has a scuff mark on the heel. Any chance you could fix that for me?"

He rolled his eyes and made his head shimmy in feigned ecstasy. "You know I'm the scuff-mark king. Let's have it."

She dug out the boot. "In the meantime I'm going to have a nice, long soak in the tub."

Alexandra could hear her grandfather whistling as she sprinkled bubble-bath crystals into the stream of water filling the bathtub. It was so nice to have Tommy back in her life. She might have lost seven years with him, but she was determined not to lose any more—or let anything interfere with what time was left to them.

Why did the image of Evan Daniels come to mind with that thought? Maybe because the last man she had been involved with had harbored ill feelings about Tommy and her background.

But there was no chance of Evan Daniels becoming a problem. After all, she wasn't involved with him. She was just having herself a mild flirtation.

Except that going to dinner with the owner of Tommy's Breguet watch—a man in the same league as her ex-husband—was risky. Evan would hold her in scorn just the way Curtis had, if he knew the truth about her background—the truth about Tommy.

Except that Alexandra was already married to Curtis by the time he found out. Big mistake, keeping her roots a secret; she'd learned that lesson the hard way.

But having dinner with a man was no crime, Alexandra reasoned as she got out of the tub and dried off. She simply wouldn't let herself become involved. She slipped back into her bedroom where her new dress was spread out on the bed.

Charcoal-gray knit, the dress had a turtleneck, dolman sleeves and a skirt that fell to midcalf. She remembered trying it on in the store. It draped around her body just right, felt and looked great with the bright accents of the red belt and boots that were high enough to disappear beneath the skirt. The only thing it hadn't done in the dressing room was call her a liar the way it did now as she stood looking at it.

Because there was nothing simple about this dinner with Evan Daniels.

And she had a feeling she was already involved.

"Tommy?" Alexandra called from the bathroom where she stood in front of the mirror applying a touch of mascara half an hour later. "Do you know what I've been craving for days, now? Your spaghetti with those weird mushrooms. There's a gourmet market across town that carries them. I was thinking that you could go and get them tonight and make the sauce tomorrow. If you leave right now, you'd be back in time for the early news you like to watch.''

"That spaghetti does sound good, doesn't it? But I don't have to go to the market tonight. I'll go in the morning and still have time to make the sauce.''

"Do you have plans for tonight?'' she asked hopefully, seeing that getting him out of the house before Evan picked her up was not going to be easy.

"I have a new novel from the book club I joined. I'm going to make myself a big bowl of popcorn and read.''

Alexandra felt guilty for needing to disrupt his plans. But it was for his own good. Just in case he knew that Evan owned the watch, she didn't want him to find out that was who her date was with. "You know what happens when you spend an evening like that—you fall asleep twenty minutes after your start reading and then wake up and can't sleep the rest of the night.''

"I've been drinking coffee all day, so I'm in no danger of falling asleep.''

She knew when she'd hit a dead end. Perhaps a different route. "Bingo! Why not play a little bingo first? You haven't gone there in two days. Then you could read when you get back, sort of break up a long evening.''

"The parlor is closed today—something about a broken water pipe.''

"How about a movie? You haven't been to a single movie since you got here.''

"How about I make myself a big bowl of popcorn and read my new book? Something wrong with that, Alexandra?

He was suspicious, and she couldn't blame him. "No. Nothing wrong with that at all," she lied, dusting her cheeks with a little blush and admitting defeat. Maybe she could watch for Evan to drive up, and run out to his car before he could get to the house.

But her hair didn't work. She fumbled the first attempt to French-braid it and had to do it over again. Under different circumstances she might even have done it a third time to make it slightly more perfect; but thinking to head Evan off at the pass she left it and hurried back into her bedroom. She put on her belt and then grabbed a boot. That was when the doorbell rang.

"Let it be the paperboy," she whispered as she plunged her foot into the soft red leather.

"I'll get it!" Tommy called.

"*Please* let it be the paperboy." She pulled on the second boot as fast as she could. Then she grabbed her purse and nearly ran for the living room just as she heard Evan's deep, distinctive voice.

"Hi!" she said—too loudly, too brightly, too quickly. Evan was standing in the entranceway with her grandfather, but she didn't even pause as she walked between them to the door. "I'm all ready. We can get going."

Tommy frowned at her as if she'd lost her mind, and held out his hand to Evan. "I'm The Great T. C. Dewberry."

Oh, no! Alexandra groaned inside. Leave it to Tommy to introduce himself like that. And with a straight face.

Evan accepted her grandfather's hand, smiling congenially at the older man. "I'm Evan Daniels."

"Well, I'm starved," Alexandra put in before the words were completely out of Evan's mouth. "I won't be late, Tommy, but don't wait up if you get tired.'' She made a beeline out the door, hoping Evan's impeccable manners would force him to follow. She breathed a sigh of relief when he did just that.

"Good night!" Tommy said from the doorway.

"You didn't tell me you were living with someone," Evan teased as they headed for his sleek black sports car.

"Tommy is my grandfather," she answered simply, as she got in and he closed the door.

"It isn't that I doubt that he deserves the title, but why is he *The Great* T. C. Dewberry?" Evan asked as he slipped behind the wheel and started the car.

Here we go, Alexandra thought. Maybe she shouldn't tell him the truth, she offered herself. Maybe she should make up some lie about Tommy being eccentric. But what was the point? In fact, maybe it was better to tell Evan the truth. He'd be turned off by it and she'd be saved from herself.

Alexandra took a deep breath and stared steadfastly out the windshield rather than watch Evan's reaction. "I told you before that my grandfather had taught me locksmithing—that was his trade. But there wasn't enough flair in that to suit him, so he became a carnival performer and then the owner of a small one of his own. 'The Great T. C. Dewberry' is what he called himself. He put his knowledge of locks to use and, in his heyday, rivaled Houdini for his escapes. Not to mention his escapades," she added under her breath.

"You're kidding?"

"It's the absolute truth."

Evan laughed. "That's wonderful."

Wonderful? Had she heard him right? Alexandra glanced at him, and sure enough, his face beamed with delight. "You don't find that...creepy?" Maybe he was covering up. But she'd become adept at seeing through people who were polite enough to try, and Evan seemed to honestly find this amusing.

"Why should I find it creepy?"

"Carnivals are not the most respected forms of entertainment in this country. General consensus is that the people who work them are sleazy transients at best and con artists and criminals at worst. Finding it creepy is one of the more mild reactions I've run into."

"Is that why you didn't want me to pick you up at your house and why you were in such a hurry to get me out once I was there? Did you think that your grandfather would tell me before you could?"

It was as good a reason as the real one. It had happened before. "Something like that."

He shook his head and chastised her. "Well, you had me pegged wrong, lady. I think your grandfather being a carnival performer is great. Why don't you use that angle to advertise Security Systems? Seems to me that someone good at picking locks would be a terrific consultant for a security business. You could say you have an expert giving you advice. You could even let him try to break in without tripping your alarms, to prove how safe you've made a place."

"You'd like Tommy. You think alike," she said, still surprised by Evan's reaction and the fact that it seemed genuine. "My grandfather is convinced that any association with him would be a good angle, too. But I decided it was better to build my business on my own merits. I didn't want the image of a carnival atmosphere or anything shady connected with a company intended to offer security."

Evan glanced at her. "So it isn't only other people who see the carnival connection as shady. It sounds as if you do, too."

"I never thought it was shady, no. I grew up traveling with Tommy's carnival, and I loved it and him too much to ever see it that way. It's just that I've run into that opinion often enough in my life to know it's pretty common."

"Well, you haven't run into it here."

But I would have if you knew the whole story. Rather than get into any more, she changed the subject. "So, where are we going?"

"Do you like Italian food?"

"I love it," she said, recalling how her feeble scheming had arranged an Italian feast for the very next day.

"Great, because we have reservations right here at Three Sons," he said as he pulled into the parking lot and stopped the car. "And I'm glad you're starving. I hate to take a woman out to dinner and have her pick at her food."

He got out, and as he came around the front of the car Alexandra took stock of him for the first time tonight. He wore a dove-gray suit that rode every line of his body with the liquid perfection of expensive fabric and the finest tailoring. Beneath the jacket a pale pink shirt peeked around a charcoal-colored tie with tiny pink polka dots on it. Tall and lean, cleanly shaven, his hair shining and wavy, he was strikingly attractive, and Alexandra's gaze was glued to him even as he opened her door.

Once she'd gotten out she waited while he locked the car; but instead of watching what he was doing, he looked at her. "I haven't had a chance to tell you how terrific you look tonight."

She thanked him for the compliment and then forgot to return it when he placed his hand at her lower back to steer her into the restaurant. Warm waves radiated from the spot he touched and for a moment Alexandra felt as if she might just melt. By the time she had regained her calm they were seated at a linen-covered table in the midst of vivid Romanesque decor, and the moment for telling him how good he looked seemed to have passed.

With her permission he ordered for them both and after their Burgundy was served, Alexandra said, "I read about your investment firm in the newspaper. Whoever wrote the article seemed to think you're going to single-handedly help the economy."

He laughed. "I don't know about that. But we have provided a few new jobs with the opening of the Denver office."

"Is business good?"

"I can't complain."

And apparently he didn't want to talk shop. "How did you start collecting watches...and clocks?" she asked in hopes of hitting a topic he was more likely to expand on.

"I've had a fascination for them since I was a little kid," he said after their salads were served. "There wasn't a watch or a clock anywhere in our house that I didn't get around to taking apart at one point or another.

"Unfortunately I was no good at putting them back together, so my father started coming home with ones he'd pick up cheap at flea markets or thrift shops. Most of what he brought home was dime-store junk, but occasionally he'd bring me something that wasn't valuable but that would strike me as beautiful. Then I wouldn't have the heart to open it up and mess with the workings. Those I'd put away and take out now and then, just to look at. After a while I started having more watches in shoe boxes and clocks on a shelf in my closet than what I took apart. And that was how the collection started.''

''And the more prosperous you got, the more expensive the pieces you collected?'' she asked as their pasta marinara was served.

''Not necessarily. There were a few I bought before I could afford them. My third year in college, I spent a semester's worth of rent money on a clock and had to sleep in my car.''

He smiled at the reminiscence, and Alexandra's glance slipped down the off-center slope of his lips. Tasting her pasta was a lifeline that pulled her back from fantasy when she realized clocks were the last thing on her mind. ''Oh, this is wonderful,'' she said of the mushroom-laden marinara, thinking that he was, too.

''I'm glad you like it. It's one of my favorites.''

After a second bite she asked, ''Is there a story that goes with the acquisition of any of your watches?''

''You mean like an international bidding war or something I got from a midnight meeting in an alley? No, nothing that interesting.''

''What about that gold pocket watch with the notches in the case?''

''The Breguet. My personal favorite. I don't know why the notches are in it. They were all made by a jeweler, so they were put in intentionally but not by Breguet himself, and I don't have any idea why.''

Alexandra reached for her wineglass, studying its delicate stem. "Maybe they marked each passage as it went from generation to generation."

"It's possible."

"How did you come by it?"

"It was a gift. That's why it means the most to me. My father gave it to me a week before he died five years ago."

Then Evan's father must have bought it from Wizencrantz, Alexandra thought. "Do you ever sell pieces out of the collection?"

"I haven't, no. But offers come in every now and then. In fact, one came in recently on the Breguet. Unfortunately the letter was mangled in the mail, envelope and all. I could barely piece together what watch was being asked about, but the name of whoever wrote it and most of the return address were gone so I couldn't even let them know it wasn't for sale."

Alexandra's pasta didn't seem to want to go down. She took a drink of water. "A recent offer on the Breguet? Do you mind my asking how much?"

"Sixty thousand. But it's appraised value is higher."

"Sixty thousand," she repeated so it would sink into her spinning thoughts.

"The money doesn't matter," Evan went on. "That's one piece I'll never consider selling. It has too much sentimental attachment for me. That one, I want to pass down to my own kids if I'm ever lucky enough to have any. Maybe I'll make a notch where the others leave off and begin a tradition of my own."

"I wonder where the letter came from?" she mused, unable to ignore the unsettled feeling she had.

"As I said, it was impossible to tell. The only part of the address we could make out was the zip code."

"I don't suppose you remember what it was?" she ventured, as if she were walking into a dark cave and expected bats to fly out at her at any moment.

Evan finished his wine. "I don't remember the numbers, but Brian said it was from Canon City—he must have looked it up out of curiosity. Are you okay?" Evan asked. "The light in here is dim, but all of a sudden you look really pale. Is the marinara too rich for you?"

Alexandra shook her head, both to his question and to her own thoughts. What she was thinking just plain couldn't be. Could it?

No, it couldn't.

"I'm fine, and the marinara is out of this world," she answered finally.

Evan accepted that and went on to talk about other watches and clocks in his collection. He told her stories about what had inspired him to buy some of them and various offers he'd had to sell them over the years. When they had both finished eating he sat back. "I've monopolized this conversation. Let it be a lesson to you never to get me started talking about the collection."

"I didn't mind," she said honestly. "It's all very interesting." Or maybe it was just that he was. But either way, it had kept her mind off that Canon City postmark on the offer for the Breguet, and for that she was grateful.

"How about you? What obsesses you besides burglar alarms?"

"Like hobbies, you mean?" How dull it sounded to admit she didn't have any, that work was the sum and substance of her life. "I like to read and watch TV." She listed the only things she could come up with, realizing that since Curtis, she'd purposely filled her life with work and entertainments she could do alone. Then she thought of the few times she socialized. "And sometimes John and I go to the movies or an occasional concert at Red Rocks," she finished, hoping that by adding John she sounded less like the loner she'd become over the years since the carnival had been sold and she'd lost Tommy and her husband at the same time.

"John?" Evan asked, raising his perfect eyebrows into questioning arcs over those midnight-blue eyes.

Just then the waitress removed their plates and asked if they would care for dessert. When Alexandra declined, Evan said, "No, thanks. I'm just having coffee and jealousy." He looked straight at Alexandra. "You told me you didn't have a 'significant other' and I thought I had a clear field."

"You do," she answered, her mouth once more working faster than her brain. "I mean, John is a friend, or more like a big brother, really. His mother was part of Tommy's carnival so we grew up together, were tutored together, played together. We even learned locksmithing together from Tommy. When Tommy and I settled in Colorado, John stayed, too. He said he was tired of moving to a different place every week and wanted roots for once in his life. He's still just like family."

"Oh, I see. Your counterpart to Brian."

"Did you two grow up together?"

"Right next door. Then we shared a dorm room at college and an apartment when we got our first jobs—until Brian moved into a place with a girlfriend. But even then, he was only one floor up. Seems like we've always been in each other's hip pockets. As you said, just like family." Evan paid the check and came around to pull out Alexandra's chair. "It's nice to meet someone with the same kinds of ties and loyalties I have. I'm afraid I'm short on patience for people who always think of themselves first and can't be bothered to put any energy into close relationships."

Alexandra agreed with him as they left the restaurant. Once in his car, Evan didn't immediately start the engine. Instead he angled toward her slightly, stretching his arm along the back of the seat and resting his hand so near that she thought she could feel the heat of it. "Would you like to go dancing?"

She made a face. "I hate to admit it but I don't dance."

He grinned. "Good. Because I'm lousy at it. I just didn't want the evening to end yet."

She didn't, either. And the very fact of how much she didn't want it to end was a warning to her. "It's getting late, though, and tomorrow is a workday for me. Maybe we should call it a night."

"Now I'm sorry I didn't order that three-course dessert, after all," he said as he finally started the car.

They didn't say much on the way home, which gave Alexandra the opportunity of watching him from the corner of her eye. His face wasn't as male-model perfect as she remembered his friend's to be, but there was such strength and raw masculinity in it that she couldn't help liking it better than Brian's fashion-model perfection. His high, prominent cheekbones, sharp jawline, and a firm, square chin gave him a rugged-looking face; yet he didn't look so rugged that he couldn't wear a suit elegantly. And he had a great neck—just corded enough to give him an athlete's look. Curtis had had such a scrawny neck....

"Would you mind turning down the heat a little?" she asked, surprised by the breathiness of her voice.

"It isn't on," Evan replied. "But we can have a little fresh air if you're too warm." He pushed a button on the control panel on his door and lowered the back windows just enough so the evening air could come in.

"It must have been the wine," she said by way of explanation, knowing all the while that it was really Evan Daniels who had gone to her head and upped her temperature.

When he pulled into her driveway Alexandra was at once relieved and disappointed. Should she risk inviting Evan in?

His hand rode her back all the way to the porch and stayed while she searched her purse for her key.

"Will you be coming by the house tomorrow?" Evan asked.

"I don't usually oversee the installation, no. I have complete confidence in John."

"It wasn't quality control I was thinking about."

Alexandra found her keys and glanced up at him. The yellow glow of the light Tommy had left on for her washed Evan's features. He was smiling that smile that had the power to send little skitters all along her nerve endings, and it didn't help that he was closer than she had thought.

"I was just wondering when I'm going to see you again," he went on.

Those little skitters turned into sparks. Encountering him for business purposes was acceptable, after all. It was within the boundaries of admiration-from-afar fantasy. "I'll stop by to see how things are going," she said, her voice so husky she didn't recognize it.

"Great," he responded with the same quality in his voice.

Slowly he leaned nearer and Alexandra stretched up on her toes without even thinking about it; he was going to kiss her good-night, and she was glad.

Then his lips were on hers, warm and firm, and the scent of his after-shave was all around her. He pulled her closer with his hand at the base of her spine and laid the palm of his other one along her jaw, holding her to the kiss with a gentle strength.

She raised her hand to his chest, finding that his suit coat had a silky texture but that what lay beneath it was hard and powerful. His lips parted just slightly. His breath was warm against her cheek and she could have stayed like that for days and days.

But slowly she came back to reality and eased away from his kiss and then from him.

"Thanks for dinner," she whispered unsteadily, even though she had intended to sound in control.

"I'll see you tomorrow," he answered, giving her one last, light kiss before sliding his hand down her jawline in a caress she wanted to feel on more places than her face.

Alexandra watched him go back to his car, start the engine and leave. But she didn't enter the house right away. Instead she waited in the autumn air until she had cooled off.

Chapter Four

Coincidences were on Alexandra's mind most of the sleepless night and the next morning as she dressed in jeans and a hunter-green sweater.

Sometime around two in the morning she'd accepted as coincidence—again—Security Systems's being hired to install an alarm to protect a collection that included the Breguet watch. It was plausible that Brian had seen the interview and suggested her company, she conceded, and that it had nothing whatsoever to do with Tommy.

But the coincidence she was having more difficulty accepting was that the mangled letter offering to buy the watch had come from Canon City. Canon City was where Tommy had been for the past seven years.

But the offer was for sixty thousand dollars. Did Tommy have that much money? Could his savings have grown to such an amount in only seven years? That was hard to believe. Possible, she admitted as she brushed her hair and caught it in a loose ponytail halfway down her back, but hard to believe, all the same.

Maybe Tommy had somehow met a watch collector in Canon City. Maybe he had talked about the Breguet and put someone else on the trail of it. After all, the watch had been one of her grandfather's favorite topics of conversation. And collectors could be encountered anywhere.

Besides, she thought as she headed out of her bedroom, if Tommy had written the letter and received no answer by now, he'd have followed up with a phone call or another letter. He wasn't a shrinking violet, after all. And if he was seriously determined to get the watch back again, a little thing like no answer to one letter wouldn't stop him.

No. This might be a more far-reaching coincidence than Security Systems's being hired to install an alarm to protect the Breguet; but it was still just that—a coincidence.

Tommy was dusting the living room when Alexandra went through it to the kitchen. He was humming along with a recording of "Singing in the Rain" and dancing from end table to television to bookcase with the panache of Gene Kelly.

"Good morning, darling," he interrupted his music to say, picking up the song the minute she'd returned his greeting.

From the kitchen door Alexandra watched him for a moment, taking in that round bald head of his, his red sweater with the white ascot tucked into the V neckline, his natty tweed slacks and highly polished loafers. He had long since accepted the loss of the watch, she told herself.

In the kitchen, she filled a bowl with cereal and milk and then stood against the doorjamb facing the living room to eat it.

"Why are you using a fork to eat cornflakes?" Tommy asked when his record finished and the stereo turned off automatically.

"I don't like the milk," she said between bites.

He made a shame-on-you sound with his tongue and swept aside the lace half-tier curtains on the front window to dust the sill. "Are you taking the day off?" he asked with a glance at her jeans.

"I don't have any appointments until tonight so I thought I'd just catch up on some paperwork. I have a few errands to run and then I want to look in on John to see how things are going at the job before I come back here." And she wanted to look very casual, as if seeing Evan again today were no big deal. He didn't have to know she had been up for three hours already so she could wash and curl her hair, or that she had actually ironed her jeans, of all things.

Alexandra watched as Tommy raised his dustrag to the picture of her great-grandfather and couldn't fight the urge to join him in front of it.

"I've been thinking about the watch," she began conversationally as she looked at the Breguet in the photograph. "I wonder where it is these days. Do you know?"

"I've heard a rumor or two," Tommy replied vaguely, sounding as if the subject didn't really interest him. "How was your dinner last night?"

"Good," she answered, still staring at the old photograph. "What would the Breguet be worth now, do you think?"

Tommy shrugged negligently. "What it's worth doesn't matter," he said as he spritzed the glass that protected the picture and polished it. "Never did. A family heirloom doesn't have a value in dollars and cents. It's the heritage that counts, the connection with the past, with the family that came before. Holding it in your hand, just knowing you're touching something that other generations of your family have held, connects you to those people whose blood runs in your veins but whom you've never been able to meet. Money can't buy that, darling. Nothing can buy that."

"But it could buy back the watch," she ventured, hating herself for still wondering about the author of Evan's mangled letter.

"Yes, it could do that, all right." Tommy moved on to the coffee table. "Where did you eat?"

It took her a moment to realize he was asking another question about her date. "We went to Three Sons."

"I heard they turned it into a new, fancy place."

"Mmm. Not long ago. It's beautiful."

"How long have you know this Evan Daniels?" her grandfather asked, then.

"Not long," she responded ambiguously, keeping her fingers crossed that Tommy wouldn't ask how they'd met. She'd bald-face lie to him if she had to, rather than so much as raise her grandfather's curiosity.

"What does he do for a living?"

"He owns an investment company."

Tommy fluffed the overstuffed pillows on the salmon-colored sofa. "Do you know a lot about him?"

"No, not a lot."

"But you like him, do you?"

Boy, did she. "Yes."

"What kind of a man does he seem to you?" Tommy asked as he dusted the shade on the white bean-pot lamp.

"Nice. Very nice. Great manners. Generous. Comfortable with himself. Confident. Kind. Together. Strong. Stable. Interesting. Intelligent. Personable. Good values. Moral. Easy to be with—"

Tommy cut her off, stopping his dusting to smile at her. "I take it you *really* like him."

"He's a pretty impressive man," she admitted.

The phone rang just then and Tommy dashed into her bedroom-office to answer it before the machine could click in.

Alexandra went into the kitchen and rinsed her bowl. As she did, the thought of Evan's mangled letter came back again to haunt her. Why couldn't she stop thinking about it?

Tommy didn't write that letter, she told herself yet again, firmly. If he had, it would mean he was waiting anxiously for an answer. And if that was the case, there was no way her grandfather could have discovered that her date last night was with none other than Evan Daniels and not have bombarded her with questions this morning. In fact, if that was the case, Tommy would have been up when she got home.

No. Her grandfather might have heard a rumor or two about where the watch was, but he didn't know the truth. And he hadn't written the letter offering to buy it. The Canon City postmark was just another coincidence.

Evan's eggs were cold. And there wasn't too much that tasted worse than cold, overcooked eggs. He washed the mouthful down with a drink of orange juice and pushed his plate away. First he'd scorched his breakfast—with Mary doing duty at Jeannie's he'd had to fix it himself—and now he'd been too preoccupied to eat before the whole mess had gotten cold. Orange juice and coffee would have to do.

Orange juice, coffee—and thoughts of Alexandra.

He looked at his watch and wondered when she'd get here. What she'd be wearing. If that strawberry-ice hair of hers would be loose.

That hair was something. And his hands were itching to get into it. Maybe he could talk her into a horseback ride today. A fast gallop might work it free.

In his mind's eye he could suddenly see her astride Livvy, see her thighs wrapped around the horse's sides. And her hair blowing out behind her.

Livvy had a bad shoe. Why hadn't he remembered it before? There'd be no riding her until it was fixed.

He picked up his plate and took it to the kitchen, leaving it on the countertop while he made a phone call. When he hung up a few minutes later he was disappointed that the farrier couldn't get there for three days. Actually he'd been more abrupt than he needed to be with the man when he'd found out he was going to have to wait.

"Get a grip," he muttered to himself.

But ever since meeting Alexandra, that was easier said than done. The only grip he had any desire to get was on her.

Not that his attraction for her was purely physical; it just started there. He was impressed with the rest of her, too. She didn't put on airs or seem to be into game playing. With her, he had the feeling that what he saw was what he was getting and he liked that. It was a great change from what he'd been running into lately.

And what he saw was an interesting, independent woman who had all the earmarks of loyalty, unselfishness, and high ethics, along with enough femininity to temper it all and turn him inside out without half trying.

Evan went through the living room into the collection room where John and his men were just setting up to go to work. When they had exchanged the amenities Evan said, "I have to run to the post office, so if Alexandra comes by while I'm gone will you keep her here for me? Tell her I want to talk to her."

"Is there something I can do?" John asked.

Evan shook his head. "I just don't want to miss her and I have to overnight-express some papers to my New York office."

"Alexandra doesn't usually check up on us."

"I know, she told me. But I asked her to come."

John frowned at him and Evan wasn't sure if the blond man doubted him or saw Evan's attraction to Alexandra and was feeling protective. "Alexandra said you've been friends since you were kids," he remarked, to break the ice and to see if John's feelings for her were as platonic as she'd claimed hers were for John. "She told me you'd traveled together with her grandfather's carnival, that Tommy had taught you both to be locksmiths."

John's frown changed to raised eyebrows. "She told you about the carnival?"

"I thought it was great."

"She doesn't tell that to just anybody."

"No, I don't imagine she does. Anyway, she said the two of you were like brother and sister."

"We have been, yeah."

"Well, she thinks highly of you. Almost as highly as I think of her," he went on to put John's mind at ease if he felt protective toward Alexandra. Or maybe to let the other man know his intentions, just in case John's feelings for her weren't entirely brotherly. "I'll be back shortly," he said, and then left. Every man for himself. . . .

"The client wants to see you," John greeted Alexandra the minute she arrived. "He said to have you wait."

"I need to see him, too." And not just for personal reasons. "I want to upgrade the system," she informed her friend as she filched one of the doughnut holes he was eating with his midmorning coffee.

"Why?" John asked around a cheekful of one of them, his tone indicating he thought she was crazy.

"I just think a backup unit is a good idea."

John chewed his food and swallowed before saying, "But the contracts are signed, Alexandra. And it'll cost more."

"I'll have to absorb the extra expense. It was my oversight—I should have recommended the system with a backup in the beginning. May I have a grape?"

"You can have anything you want, but don't change the game plan at this late date."

Alexandra took the grape, wondering as she did why she was eating when she wasn't hungry. "I have to," she said simply.

"The system we agreed on is sensitive enough for this size room. We aren't wiring Fort Knox. The alarm rings directly in to the police, and you know their average response time in this area is under three minutes. Why do you think there needs to be a backup?''

"I'd just feel better about it. I've already called the supplier and they have a unit in stock. I'll go by there to pick it up this afternoon and bring it back here so you guys don't lose any time doing it. I just wanted you to know so you could drill more holes and prepare for the extra installation.''

"This is going to cost you an arm and a leg.''

"I know you worry about me, John, but it'll be okay. The main thing I wanted out of this job was to catch up on your back pay. Absorbing the extra cost will just mean I break even instead of making a profit. At this point I'd rather lose the profit and know I did this job right.''

"Lose the profit? What are you talking about?''

Alexandra recognized the deep voice that came from the doorway behind her, and goose bumps erupted up and down her arms. She turned to watch Evan coming into the room, taking in the second-skin fit of time-faded jeans and a navy football jersey whose sleeves were pushed up to his elbows. "I want to upgrade the system. The primary alarm is actually the one we agreed on, but this has a backup, in case the first one fails or is bypassed.''

Evan frowned slightly. "And this other system is more sensitive?''

"A lot,'' John put in under his breath, barely loud enough to be heard.

"It was my oversight. I just didn't realize until you were talking about your collection last night how valuable some of your pieces are. I should have been more thorough, and since it was my mistake we'll install the additional unit at the same price.''

"The original plan seemed sufficient to me when we first talked," Evan said.

His eyes were almost the same color as the football jersey and his hair was slightly tousled from the autumn wind. Alexandra had an image of him as he must have looked in college.

"I still think it's sufficient," John said, breaking into Alexandra's thoughts.

"We don't want 'sufficient.' We want 'secure.' It will only mean a few more lasers—some coming from the ceiling and some around the windows and the door-frame, in addition to the extras along the base of the walls. And there will be some floor sensors under the carpet that no one will even know are there."

John frowned down at his coffee, his expression continuing to let it be known that he didn't agree.

"I really don't think it's necessary, Alexandra," Evan insisted.

"You may be right. But extra protection never hurt anything. Better safe than sorry," she replied, quoting one of Tommy's often-used phrases.

Evan laughed a little and shook his head. Then he glanced over at John. "I'm betting that once she's made up her mind it's a waste of energy to try fighting it. Am I right?"

"You'd win that one," John confirmed.

Evan looked again at Alexandra. "Okay, put in your backup—but I'll pay for it."

"That wouldn't be right." Alexandra saw John roll his eyes at her words.

Evan took ahold of her chin and tipped her face up, leaning down so that his own was near enough for her to smell his after-shave. In measured tones he said, "You'll find when you get to know me better that I can hold my own in the determination department. For now, you'll just have to take my word for it. I will pay for the additional system and for the labor to install it. Or you won't put it in."

Putty. She was putty in his hands. All she could think of was how good he smelled, how striking was the contrast between the midnight blue of his irises and the nearly fluorescent white around them, how sexy was the difference between the way a man's skin looked up close and the way a woman's did, and how much she wanted to repeat the kiss that had come from being this near to him last night on her porch.

Alexandra swallowed and fought for strength. "You can pay for the parts," she managed, her tone only making half the grade.

"I'll pay for parts and labor, too," he reiterated, enunciating each word.

If she didn't get out of his grip and away from the powerful attraction she felt for him, if she didn't get some air soon, Alexandra was afraid she might completely lose her calm. "There won't be any notable difference in labor," she insisted just the same.

When Evan turned to look at John, Alexandra got a close-up and personal view of his ear. His ear! for crying out loud, and her heart was beating harder.

"Is that right?" Evan asked of her friend.

"We pay labor by the day, and no, it won't take any extra days to install.

Evan's face came back her way. "Okay, then. It's a deal."

He gave a little pulse of his hand around her jaw-bone before he slid it away, leaving Alexandra with a tingling sensation that felt a lot like physical longing. "Good," she said, trying hard for the semblance of a businesslike tone in her voice. "I'll go pick up everything now."

Evan took ahold of her arm. "Not until I write you a check to cover it."

"I'll be back sometime this afternoon," she said over her shoulder to John as she left the room.

With check in hand she was beside her car ten minutes later. Evan stretched his arm along the roof and leaned on the open door as she got in. "Since we're both dressed for it, how about fast-food hamburgers in the park for dinner tonight? This good weather could disappear any minute and it would be a shame to waste it."

Alexandra knew she was dancing barefoot near flame but she couldn't resist him. Not with her heart still pounding and her skin still tingling, and him grinning down at her. *Oh, you're in trouble, Dunbar.* Then she remembered the message John had greeted her with when she'd come in earlier. "Was there some problem before? John said you wanted to talk to me."

"The problem was that I was afraid I'd miss you and I didn't want to take that chance. So, what do you say to burgers in the park?"

That it sounded as good to her as a flight on the Concorde to Paris for haute cuisine. But that wasn't what she said. "I have an appointment to give a bid on an alarm system for a house in Littleton tonight at eight," she hedged, knowing she should refuse his invitation and yet wasn't able to.

"We'd have to make it early, anyway—before it gets too dark to really enjoy the leaves," Evan reasoned. "I was hoping for a long evening, but I'll settle for just dinner and letting you get to your appointment afterward if I have to."

"Okay." When had she gotten so weak-willed? she wondered. But she knew the answer. It happened the minute she'd met this man.

"I'll pick you up."

At least tonight she had a good excuse. "I have to come back with the materials anyway. I'll just make it late in the day and we can go from here."

"Perfect." He winked at her, reminding her of Tommy.

But even thoughts of her grandfather and a fresh wave of common sense telling her she shouldn't be doing this didn't matter. She wanted to be with this man and, for now at least, for a little while, she was going to be. She'd just keep him and the watch in one compartment of her life and Tommy in another.

It was a particularly colorful Indian summer, the best Denver had seen in years. The leaves on the oak trees were honey gold and jonquil yellow—so bright they looked as if they'd been plugged in and lit electrically. The cottonwoods and elms offered burnt oranges in contrast. All together, nature was in an awesome frenzy of autumnal splendor.

"This is my favorite time of year," Alexandra told Evan as they walked from their separate cars to a picnic table beside a small brook that ran through the suburban park. Evan brushed fallen leaves from the table and set the sack full of fast food there while they cleared the benches on either side of it.

"Somehow I would've guessed that of you," he answered, his deep voice resonant in the early-evening quiet of the park, which they had to themselves.

"How?" she asked dubiously, enjoying the sight of him in those same tight jeans and football jersey, now covered with a leather bomber jacket that hugged his broad shoulders like an old friend. The waning light of the sun as it neared the mountains gleamed off his wheaten hair and gilded it the same color as the brightest of the leaves.

"Your skin is so fair it's easy to see that you'd burn instead of tan. . . .

"So I'm betting you avoid it and aren't crazy about summer. The shade of your hair seems to blend in with the colors the trees are turning—sort of a mixture of the reds and umbers, but diffused through early-morning fog to give it just a highlight of pink. Add that soft blue of your eyes—the color of the sky now that the sun isn't blazing through it—and there's just something calm and peaceful and quietly dignified about you, like this time of year."

He said it all so matter-of-factly that he managed to boost her ego without embarrassing her. Alexandra sat on the bench and divvied up the burgers and fries from the white paper sack, setting out Evan's coffee with his three double cheeseburgers and putting the tea bag in her own hot water. "What's your favorite time of year?" she asked him.

Evan swung a booted foot over the bench on the other side of the table and sat down. He lifted the lid of his coffee, took a sip and then closed it again to keep it hot. "I'm a fall-and-winter person, too. Spring is okay, but short and strange with halfhearted snow that's trying to be rain. Summer feels too frenzied and I'm not crazy about the heat. Besides, I've always thought summer is a tougher time to be single and un-attached."

Alexandra buttoned her jean jacket against the chill of a breeze. "Why is that?"

He finished chewing a bite of his hamburger with a cocked, close-lipped smile. "It must have something to do with my annual craving to go to Disneyland. Without kids to take, it just doesn't seem worth it."

"I've never been to Disneyland, so I can't say I crave going." She dipped a fry into some catsup and watched the exaggerated shock that crossed his face.

"You've never been to Disneyland? You must have had a deprived childhood."

That made her laugh. "Hardly. You forget that I grew up in a carnival!"

"Still, everyone should see Disneyland. It's more a work of art than anything else. As soon as I have kids, I'm making a standing reservation for once a year."

"You are a strange man. No wonder you thought my being attached to a carnival was nifty," she teased, even though this was just one more thing that made her like him. She lifted the cover of her paper cup to see if her tea had steeped long enough; it hadn't so she replaced it. "I guess I know what you mean about summer being a harder time to be single and alone, though. There's such a laid-back, casual feeling to it that you want to be with people you know well and feel comfortable with. And it does seem like there's a lot going on that I'm not doing."

He reached over and stole one of her French fries. It was a gesture of familiarity that for some reason Alexandra liked.

"Have you ever been married?" he asked.

"Mmm." She swallowed a bit of burger. "But it hardly counts. I only made it a little more than a year."

"Divorced?"

"Yup." And she didn't want to go into the details. "What about you?"

"Never married or divorced."

"You're a confirmed bachelor?" She borrowed his coffee stirrer to retrieve the tag on the end of her tea bag so she could take it out of her cup.

"A confirmed bachelor? Not on your life. My sister is married and Brian will be next month and I'm jealous as hell. How am I going to get those kids to take to Disneyland every year if I don't get married?"

"That does present a problem," she agreed, laughing at him. "So, if you want to be married and have kids so badly—how come you aren't and don't?"

"It's not a pretty picture," he said, feigning a frown. "Lucky in investments, unlucky in love."

Alexandra laughed at him. "Meaning you've been a workaholic and the right woman didn't trip you so you'd notice her along the way."

"Guilty as charged. But all that has changed."

He stared directly into her eyes as he said that and her heart gave a giant leap. She moored it back down with some effort and changed the subject. "You have a sister?"

Leaving half of his third burger, Evan tossed the wrappings into the empty sack and uncovered his coffee. Then he angled slightly on the bench and brought his boot up so his knee could support his elbow. "Jeannie. She's a year younger than I am and she just made me the uncle of a bouncing baby girl a couple of days ago."

"Congratulations! Any other family?"

"Our mother retired to San Diego with her closest sister. There are also numerous and sundry distant relatives scattered around."

The breeze rearranged his hair, tousling it and leaving a wave across one side of his forehead. Alexandra had the strongest urge to reach over and smooth it back again, even though it just made him look more ruggedly handsome. Belatedly she realized he'd asked her about her family—if there was anyone but her grandfather.

"No, there's just Tommy and me."

"Why do you call him Tommy?"

"It's shorter than The Great T. C. Dewberry." That made him laugh and not only did Alexandra revel in the sound of it rumbling from deep in his chest, but she enjoyed the creases and crinkles it made at the corners of those dark blue eyes and around his mouth. "Tommy never liked being called anything else. And he was right. There was something just too ordinary about Grandpa or Grandfather to fit him."

For a moment Evan watched her through the cloud of steam that rose from his cup as he drank his coffee. There was something between them, she reflected; something strong and almost tangible it was so intense. Was this what "chemistry" was? If so, she'd never experienced anything quite like it.

"Were you hurt by your divorce, or was it something you wanted?" he asked then, seriously.

Alexandra shrugged. "I was hurt. But I'm okay now."

That must have been the answer he was looking for, because he smiled.

"What about you? Has being unlucky in love hurt you?" she asked.

"A couple of times. But nothing too debilitating. I'm not carrying any baggage."

"No, I didn't notice any when you got out of your car," she teased.

"Do you want to marry again?"

Loaded question. Did she want to marry again? She'd love to. Did she believe she could? No. Would she put herself and Tommy in line for a second round of what had happened with Curtis? Absolutely not.

The breeze caught their debris-filled bag and swept it to the end of the table. Alexandra lunged and caught it before it spilled and then glanced at her watch in the waning daylight. "I'd better head for the hills," she said rather than answer his question. "I have to go home and change into something more businesslike and get to my appointment."

"You could cancel it. I have a phone in the car."

She shook her head. "I've had to reschedule with this lady three times already. I have to go." And besides, thoughts of her marriage and what had come of it were good reminders that she'd put her life on another course she'd better stick to.

Evan took the sack and threw it in a trash can. Then he draped his arm across her shoulders and they headed for their cars, and somehow it felt as natural and as familiar as if he'd been doing it forever.

"I have to leave tomorrow for a week in New York," he said, his tone conveying a clear reluctance to go. "But when I get back I want to spend more time with you."

There in the curve of his arm the autumn breeze didn't seem as cool, and her reasons for not getting in any deeper with him didn't seem as important. "I don't know," she mused, her tone light, because she couldn't quite bring herself to refuse what she knew she should. "Your system will be in by then, and after I teach you how to operate it—"

"You'll have to see me just because you want to." He cut her off, finishing her sentence.

"Assuming, of course, that I do want to," she teased, wondering where she'd learned to flirt like this when she'd never done it before.

They reached her car and Evan swung around in front of her, his nearness nudging her back against the door. "Do you want to?"

More than anything. "This has been pretty nice," she admitted, glancing at the arching branches overhead.

"Then you'll see me again?"

She took a deep breath and told herself to say no, or to at least put him off. Her attraction to him was rapidly turning into something stronger. And there were just too many complications; too many things he didn't know and wouldn't like when he found out.

But being with him, hearing him say the right things, drinking in the sight of him, having every nerve ending in her body brought to life by a single touch—all had the elements of a fantasy realized.

"Yes, I'd like to see you again," she said. And this time her mind and her mouth were in communion.

His smile was slow and satisfied. "Good."

He leaned his arms on the roof of her car and lowered his lips to hers. Warm and tasting of coffee and autumn air, they parted almost the moment they touched hers. Alexandra answered him in kind. She reached one hand to the soft leather of his jacket where it rested against his chest and laid the other on the side of his neck, feeling the heat and hardness there.

His lips parted more. Just the tip of his tongue spread hers a bit wider and then wider still, until he could come inside freely. He followed the line of her front teeth and dipped farther in where Alexandra met him with her own tongue, matching him circle for circle in a little mating dance.

He slid his arms from the car to wrap them around her, pulling her up against the full length of him. She let her own instincts prevail to slip her arm inside his coat and around his broad back while her other hand went from the side of his neck to the nape where she tangled her fingers in his hair.

His mouth was wide open now and Alexandra welcomed it, lost in the feel of his arms tightly holding her, of his body pressed to hers, of his hands working the softness of her back. When had he reached under her jean jacket? She couldn't remember; all she knew was that it was nice, that she wished there wasn't even the barrier of her sweater between them.

The breeze turned into a wind that whipped a long strand of her hair loose and wrapped it around his head. A faint groan came from deep in his throat and he took one of his hands out from under her jacket to cup the back of her head, delving into her hair as if it were gold dust he wanted to sift through his fingers.

Feelings were coming alive in Alexandra. Things she hadn't felt in a long, long time. They were stronger than they'd ever been before, and a saner part of herself reminded her to exercise some control.

She drew both of her hands to Evan's chest and wedged herself away from him with enough difficulty to know that he didn't want her to go. "I have an appointment," she reminded him in a breathy voice that announced just how involved she had been in that kiss.

Evan pulled her back so that her cheek rested against his jacket and dropped his chin to the top of her head. "Sell the damn alarm system to me. I'll put it in the garage if I have to."

Alexandra laughed. "I don't think that would keep Mrs. Canzona's house burglarproof."

"She can move into my garage."

Alexandra started to laugh, but it came out more as a sigh. A disappointed sigh. "I have to go."

His muscular chest rose against her cheek with the deep breath he took. Then he exhaled and straightened away from her.

"This is going to be the longest week of my life."

"It'll pass before you know it," she told him, even though she didn't have a doubt that he was right.

He kissed her again, quickly, and then again.

"I have to go," she said in a mock shriek.

He growled and leaned around her to open the car door, waiting for her to get in. "I'll call you from New York."

"Have a safe trip."

"Want to come along?" he asked sounding as if he were only half teasing.

"I think I'd better stay here, but thanks for the offer."

He reached for the loose strand of her hair and rubbed it between his thumb and fingers. Then he ducked in for one last kiss, said "Damn" under his breath and closed her door. "Lock it and be careful," he ordered through the glass as she started the car and pulled away from the curb.

But somehow Alexandra knew that she'd stopped being careful right about the same time she'd met him.

Chapter Five

When the telephone rang the following Thursday night, Tommy beat Alexandra to answering it. Again. For the past week it had seemed as if they were racing for each call—with her grandfather winning more often than Alexandra. And rightly so, since most of the nonbusiness calls were his—just as this one was.

Alexandra sighed peevishly and glanced at the clock on her nightstand as she slipped on a cranberry-colored turtleneck sweater over tan slacks. Seven twenty-six, and still no word from Evan.

She'd talked to him only twice while he was away, though with Tommy getting as many calls as a teenager lately, she couldn't fault Evan. In fact the message he'd left last night had opened with his own frustration over either getting a busy signal or her answering machine every time he tried to reach her. Then he had asked her to leave tonight open. His plane wasn't getting in until late this afternoon and if she was free, he'd said, he'd like to see her. As an afterthought and obviously mindful of the reluctance she had shown every other time he'd wanted to be with her, he'd suggested she slot this evening to show him how to run his newly finished alarm system. He'd ended by saying he'd call as soon as he got in today.

"Please get off the phone," Alexandra whispered to herself, willing her grandfather to cut his conversation short.

As if in answer to her plea, Tommy hung up. "Okay, now. Come on, Evan," she said under her breath.

"I'm going out, Alexandra," Tommy informed her through her bedroom door.

Dressed now, and with her hair wrapped in a loose knot at the back of her head, she opened the door. "I think I have an appointment tonight, so I may have to leave while you're gone," she told her grandfather as he took his camel-hair overcoat and his homburg hat out of the hall closet and put them on.

"You work too hard," he said. "You should go out more, meet some men."

"I don't know," she teased him. "This past week it seems as if you have enough of a romance going for both of us." She'd answered the phone often enough to know that a good portion of the times the caller was that same woman who had been so anxious to speak to Tommy the morning Security Systems had started work at Evan's house. And since her grandfather was always so determined to take the calls in private, Alexandra assumed love was on the verge of blooming. She could only hope his taste in women had improved.

But Tommy didn't respond to her remark about his personal life. Instead he seemed bent on pushing for hers. "You're too young not to be painting the town red with a different man every night, darling. Or finding one to marry—not that I'm in any hurry to become a great-grandfather," he added with feigned distaste. "But one way or another, you should be out getting yourself a man. You know, there're more fish in the sea, and the best one hasn't been caught yet."

"I have you and John," she reminded. "Besides, you wouldn't want to be cleaning up after some sloppy guy and a bunch of sloppy kids, too. Think of that."

He closed his eyes, raised his busy eyebrows and smiled beatifically. "Ah, now that would be a challenge. You're too much like me—too neat. I have to search for things to clean. It's no fun at all."

Alexandra laughed. "You're nuts."

"There's a single fellow who brings his mother to play bingo. Maybe I should introduce you."

"Not on your life." Why was it so tempting to say she already had someone? She knew this attraction to Evan could only be short-lived, at best.

"Well, I'm going to start looking for a man for you," Tommy declared.

Alexandra rolled her eyes. "Where are you going to look? In the Personal ads?"

"Oh, no, not there," Tommy said in a hurry. "Those were too popular in—"

"Never mind," she cut him off, seeing that he had taken her joke seriously. "I don't want you looking for a man for me anywhere."

He finished buttoning his coat and set his hat at a jaunty angle. "Well, you can't stop me from keeping my eyes open." Then he headed for the front door. "I may be late tonight. Don't wait up."

"Have a good time." Alexandra heard the door close behind him and went back to applying blush and wishing Evan would call.

The ringing of a telephone was such a small thing to have so much hope pinned on. But this past week had dragged at a snail's crawl.

Ridiculous! she'd told herself a hundred times and repeated now. It was ridiculous to miss someone she really didn't know that well; someone who wasn't actually a part of her life. But she hadn't been able to control it. And she couldn't now.

Midway through applying anticipatory lip gloss she heard the phone ring. Even though Tommy wasn't there to race against, Alexandra dived for her bedside extension.

"Hallelujah! No busy signal and no more close personal encounters with your answering machine."

Evan's voice sent warm honey running through her. "Hi," she said simply, as if she were actually casual about his call, all the while looking up at the ceiling mouthing, "Thank you, God."

"Did you get my message last night?" Evan asked.

"I did. Are you back in Denver?"

"At home and keeping my fingers crossed that you'll come right over."

"Are you sure you want me to?" She wasn't being coy; she just wanted to hide her own anxiousness to get in her car and speed the whole way to his house. "Wouldn't you rather settle back in and put off learning how to work your alarm until you're fresh?"

"Oh, you want me to be fresh, huh?" he said mischievously.

"Rested, I meant rested," she chastised.

"Fresh and rested. What exactly did you have in mind, Dunbar?"

It was easy to tell that he was determined to be incorrigible no matter what she said. Not that Alexandra minded his teasing. Even when it had a lascivious undertone to it. "The police would send me hate mail if you didn't learn how to operate your system the right way and it went off for no good reason."

He sighed. "And I thought maybe you'd missed me enough to forget work."

She'd missed him enough to forget her own name. "I have your voice on tape as proof that the reason you wanted me to come over tonight was to teach you how to operate your alarm system."

"The woman is a workaholic. Okay, if those are the terms it has to be under—I slept on the plane the whole way back. I'm wide-awake and rarin' to go. Say you'll be here in five minutes."

"It would take fifteen if my car was already running."

"Okay, then. Fifteen."

"How about half an hour?"

"I'll be waiting."

Evan showered, shaved and changed clothes. But since he still had a quarter of an hour to kill and Brian's lights were on in the pool house he went there.

"Don't tell me—she stood you up," Brian said when he opened the door to Evan.

"She'll be here in fifteen minutes," Evan informed him as he went in, following Brian to the kitchen. Evan perched on a barstool. "Just thought I'd let you know so you can come over right away for the alarm lesson and then disappear."

"Actually, I was thinking of sticking around afterward, making an evening of it for the three of us," Brian goaded.

"Great." Evan played along. "And I'll bring the Trivial Pursuit over to the bridal suite on your wedding night so we can have a few rounds then, too."

Brian just laughed as he opened the refrigerator. "Beer?" He held up a long-necked bottle.

"No, thanks."

"See, that's the advantage of being engaged and secure. I don't have to worry about having beer on my breath when I go to pick Karla up later tonight."

"Lucky Karla."

Brian laughed and put the unopened beer back in the refrigerator, coming to lean both elbows on the counter.

Evan picked up a small hand-weight and did a few leisurely curls. "It occurred to me while I was shaving—"

"Before you doused yourself in cologne?"

"Better cologne than beer breath. It occurred to me that we talked business the whole way home from the airport and you never did answer my question about how things are in the restaurant business."

"Don't ask." Brian's expression sobered.

"Selling your stereo and the stocks didn't get you out of trouble?"

"It got us out of all the trouble I knew about at the time. Unfortunately my brother neglected to tell me about another eight thousand he borrowed to do some advertising. There's a threat to put a lien against the business for the money."

Evan grimaced and shook his head. But before he could say anything, Brian went on.

"I can't pull the plug on the place. It's doing decent business—it just hasn't been able to keep up with my brother's expensive enthusiasm and overextending. We'd both take too much of a beating to close the doors now. And with his wife pregnant, this is no time for that."

"So you need another eight thousand."

"I have some things in the works," Brian said quickly, defensively.

It was clear by his tone that he didn't want to go into it. "You know," Evan continued carefully, "that Ampris deal went through—"

"Don't." His friend cut him off. "I know that even though you didn't say it, you must have made a killing. But I won't take any part of it. I'm doing this myself."

There was an edge of hostility in Brian's tone that Evan had never heard before. He put his hands up, palms outward. "Okay," he said, trying not to take offense. He glanced at his watch and went on as if there weren't an almost tangible tension in the room. "Alexandra should be here any time. You want to come over now? Or you want me to give you a buzz when she gets here?"

Brian shook his head, staring down at his clasped hands on the bar between them rather than look Evan in the eye. "I need to call Karla and then I'll be over."

"Great. I'll see you in a few minutes, then." Evan got as far as the door before Brian stopped him.

"Look, I didn't mean to jump on you."

"It's okay. I know you're feeling a lot of pressure right now."

"Sometimes it's just tough to be in your shadow."

"I didn't know I cast one," Evan said solemnly, meaning it.

"Not consciously, you don't. I told you before, it all comes from my own hang-ups. Ego."

"Tomorrow morning you can beat the hell out of me on the racquetball court if it'll help."

Brian laughed wryly, but it eased some of the strain that had been between them. "Why do you think I re-scheduled your appointments to make time?"

Evan must have been watching for her because he was at her car door before Alexandra could stop the engine.

"You're a sight for sore eyes," he said, grinning down at her as he opened the door for her to get out.

"Funny, your eyes don't look sore." They looked midnight dark and piercing and wonderful. But then so did the rest of him. He was dressed in gray slacks and a white V-neck sweater that had to have been cash-mere, it was so soft against her skin when he put his arm around her neck and pulled her close to kiss her ear as they headed for his house.

He loosened his grip on her shoulders and Alexan-dra glanced up at him. He'd had his hair cut but not so drastically that it looked anything but neater. He was clean-shaven and she had the awful craving to run her finger along his square chin and dip into that dimple in the center.

"Have you been here since I left?" he asked as they crossed the courtyard.

"No. I haven't. I told you I don't check up on John and the guys." The feeling of his arm around her was like deep heat to sore muscles, and she had a sense of having missed him even more than she'd realized. And she had realized she missed him a lot.

"Then you're in for a surprise, because the decorator finished the place during the week. It looks like a house now instead of a furniture storage space." He opened the door for her and followed her in.

It definitely looked like a house now. A beautiful house.

One step into the entranceway and they were greeted by a bronze sculpture of a woman demurely smiling over her shoulder—its lines curved and fluid. In the living room three pale cream tweed sofas formed a U around the antique fireplace, with a rich-looking oval oak table taking up the center and two matching end tables positioned in the corners of the grouping. Along one wall were shelves where books and more sculptures shared space; along another was a long oak credenza. There were baskets of silk flowers artistically placed, and an antique Bible stand between two long, paned windows displayed an atlas so old the pages were the color of mustard.

"Very nice," Alexandra approved. "Did your decorator pick everything out?"

"I beg your pardon," he said in mock indignation. "*I* picked everything out. She just arranged it. I tend to buy whatever strikes me, without thinking about style or how it goes with anything else and then I have to pay someone to come in and put it together cohesively."

But he had such good taste, Alexandra couldn't believe it was very difficult to make it work. She stepped over to another bronze sculpture that stood sentry beside the double doors connecting with the collection room. Larger than the one in the entranceway, it was a rearing wild stallion. "These statues are really wonderful. Who is the artist?"

"My sister, Jeannie. That one and the woman in the entrance are the only things the decorator didn't place. Jeannie came in and decided where they should go before the previous owners had even moved out. She said *The Shy Woman* is to welcome my guests and give the illusion of a feminine touch. *The Stallion* is there to ward off intruders who might think about poaching something. Mostly, I think she just likes to control where her sculptures end up," he finished with such affection, it was clear he didn't mind.

"You're very close to your sister, aren't you?"

"Absolutely. In fact she claims that she has to marry me off so I'll stop using her to do what I should have a wife to take care of—like the housewarming party she's doing for me on Saturday—the one you're going to come to even if I have to kidnap you to get you here."

He wouldn't have to kidnap her. It felt too good to be with him again to deny herself. "Saturday night, huh?" She pretended to think about it.

Evan put his arm around her again and pulled her close to his side, pressing his face into her hair. "Say yes or I may be forced to keep you here as a prisoner until then."

Had she really thought that seeing him again after the week's separation might have turned things more formal between them? That because the relationship was so new they might need a period of icebreaking to get back to where they had been when he'd left? Instead, it was as if the separation had warmed what was between them, relaxed them both and let crumble some invisible barrier. Alexandra didn't understand it. She knew she should resurrect the barrier. And yet this new

closeness felt too good to harm in any way. Lord help
her, but they fit so perfectly and it felt so right to be
with him that it seemed as if they were meant to be together.

"Invitations disguised as kidnapping threats—interesting theme."

"Say you won't come so I'll have reason to prove it
isn't just a threat."

She smiled at him. "I'd love to come to your party.
Now, didn't you get me over here to teach you how to
operate your alarm system?" she reminded.

"Does the saying, 'all work and no play' mean anything to you?"

"Sure. It means things get done."

He groaned. "Let's do it, then."

"I'll call the police to warn them I'm demonstrating
so they don't send out the troops, and we can start."

He gave her an exaggerated lascivious half grin. "I'd
love to get started." Then he turned her in the direction of the kitchen and the phone there. "But since
there's only business on your mind—again—make
your call. Brian should be here by the time you hang up
and we can get this over with so we'll have the rest of
the evening to ourselves. We'll say it's to celebrate the
end of the alarm installation, since you always seem to
need an excuse," he added pointedly.

But Alexandra was all business in a hurry. "You're
having Brian in on this?"

"I told you he's my right hand," Evan reminded her.

"But you will keep the code to yourself?"

"No."

"You should," she said too emphatically. "The
fewer people who know the intricacies of the system—
especially the code that will deactivate it—the better."

"There will just be you and me and Brian."

"Me?" She shook her head firmly. "I don't want to know it. I'll show you how to set the code so that choosing the numbers is something you can do yourself, privately."

Evan smiled, but this time it was tinged with a small frown. "Are you this overanxious with all your clients? I'm betting that whether you knew the code or not, you could bypass the system if you wanted to. So what difference does it make?"

"I couldn't. And even if I could, I would never do that," she said, more than serious.

"Of course, you wouldn't. I'm just saying that it doesn't matter if you know the code."

"I don't *want* to know it."

"Okay, okay. Relax. You don't have to."

"And I don't think it's a good idea to let just anybody else know it, either. Your sister maybe, just in case something happens to you. But—"

"Would you trust John to know the code to your alarm system?"

"Yes, but—"

"But nothing. I'd trust Brian with my life. I give him access to everything. Jeannie doesn't have any reason to know how to work the alarm system, although I'll probably give her the code, too. But more often than not, Brian is here when I'm gone. He has to be able to operate the thing in my absence. Besides, I'd give him anything he wanted and he knows it. He doesn't have to steal from me."

"You're sure?"

"Positive." Evan nodded toward the phone. "Make your call, he just left the pool house."

It wasn't that she didn't trust Evan's friend, Alexandra thought a few minutes later as she followed them to the collection room. In fact she liked Brian well enough and even felt a little guilty for having advised Evan against sharing the code with him. But caution was important. Sometimes she found her clients negating the whole purpose of installing an alarm system by being too open with the intricacies of operating it. Not all thefts were committed by strangers. In fact, an alarming number of them were perpetrated by people known to the victims in one way or another.

Once inside the collection room Alexandra found that it, too, was completely organized. Three more display tables had been added and took up the center of the enormous room. The other cases were set against the walls, with space between them for the grandmother and grandfather clocks.

"Well, the police know we're on a trial run, so shall we get started?" she asked.

She began by pointing out the silver alarm tape on all the windows, as well as the wiring in the screens and the suction cups on the insides of the glass to detect any vibration. Although the pads under the carpeting couldn't be seen, she showed the two men their approximate locations, explaining that they served in the backup system as motion detectors. The electric eyes and the reflectors that would complete the circuit of the infrared beams were easy to see around the lower perimeter of the room.

"This is the panic button," she said of the device near the door on the inside. "I know you have them in the bedrooms and at various other spots throughout the house, so you're familiar with them. This one acts just the same—should both systems be bypassed or not activated and someone in the house is faced with an intruder, one push of this button will alert the police anyway.''

Alexandra stepped through the double doors out into the living room again where the master-control panel was partially hidden behind the stallion sculpture. She explained how to enter the five-digit code of Evan's choice on the numbered buttons that resembled those on a push-button telephone.

''When the system is activated, the red light in the upper left corner of the panel turns on. When the system is off, the white light below it shows you that. The same code activates and deactivates the system. And with the additional unit, the backup operates automatically. Should there be a power failure, both the main system and the backup immediately switch to a continuously recharging battery until the electricity resumes, so that if an intruder were to cut the power lines, both systems would still be operable. The whole thing is connected to the main alarm, so should it be set off, it will ring into the police station as well as activating the horn outside that will alert you and a two-block radius, and hopefully scare off anyone before they get in.'' She held her hands up, her arms open. ''And that's about it. So long as it's activated, the system is ninety-percent unbeatable.''

''Well, it's a little safer than my old shoe box,'' Evan allowed facetiously.

''Just a little,'' Brian put in with a laugh. Then, to Alexandra he said, ''Nice work.''

''Thank you, but I hope it never gets a real test.'' She turned to Evan. ''I'll go into the kitchen while you program the code and then we'll give it a trial run and wake the dead around here.''

It was half an hour later by the time the code was programmed, they'd set off the shrieking outside alarm, deactivated it to stop the noise and gotten the call from the police verifying that it had only been a test of the system. That was when Brian left and Alexandra and Evan were alone again.

"I have a bottle of champagne chilling just for this occasion," Evan told her when his friend had gone out the back door.

"Champagne? For what occasion?"

"I told you, the excuse this time is to celebrate the end of installing the system," he said in reminder of what he had teasingly told her earlier, before she'd begun her warnings about letting Brian know the code.

How long could she keep Evan and the watch in one compartment and Tommy in a separate one before the twain met and found out the truth about each other? How long before that truth ended this relationship the way it had ended her marriage and hurt her in the process?

Alexandra didn't know. She only knew that she couldn't make herself seize this moment to thank Evan for his business, leave and never see him again. She had to walk the tightrope between those two separate compartments a little longer. She had to have a little more of him before the end came.

She took a breath and plunged in. "Champagne seems extravagant to celebrate finishing something as minor as a burglar alarm, but don't expect me to turn my nose up at it."

Evan's smile erupted slowly, quizzically, almost as if he knew she had crossed some imaginary line that left her admitting to them both that she was only with him because she wanted to be. But he didn't say that. In-

THE RIGHT TIME 107

stead he said, "Make yourself comfortable and I'll be right back."

Alexandra sat on the sofa that faced the fireplace, thinking that she felt right at home and how strange that was, since the difference between her place and this was about the same as the difference between a tent and the Taj Mahal. Not that she didn't like her little house and the plain, country furniture that filled it; but there was no comparison with old oak, original sculptures, ultra-plush cream-colored carpeting, and sofas that must have cost as much as her car.

Evan slipped back through the tall oak door that separated the kitchen, carrying two champagne flutes. For the second time she took in the gray slacks and white cashmere sweater that hinted of a body beneath that no desk jockey seemed likely to own.

He handed her one of the glasses and as he did, her gaze got stuck on the light scattering of chest hair visible at the very point of the V neck of his sweater. It wasn't as if she'd never seen a man's chest before, or the hair that covered it, and yet this view of his struck her as very intimate.

Alexandra accepted the champagne and forced herself to look out at the blackness of the sky through the floor-length drapes that bordered a corner window.

"How about a fire?" he suggested, setting his glass on the coffee table and going to hunker down in front of the hearth before she could say anything.

His fresh haircut bared the strong column of his neck and Alexandra's gaze ran down it to the breadth of his shoulders and then farther, to the narrowing of his waist. His gray slacks fit his hips and rear end impeccably, and once more she had to consciously make herself look at something else in the room—this time

choosing the stallion statue and for some reason notic-
ing what she hadn't before—that it was anatomically
correct.

With her mouth suddenly very dry, Alexandra took
a sip of champagne and sank down into the supremely
soft cushions of the couch as Evan lit the fire. When it
was roaring he grabbed up his glass in one fluid movement and sat beside her—*close* beside her, stretching
his arm along the sofa back.

"To finished projects and fate," he toasted, touching her glass with his.

Alexandra sipped the bubbly liquid again. "Fate?"

"For introducing us." He smiled at her—a crooked,
heart-stoppingly charming smile that raised only one
side of his mouth and drew the dimple in his chin off
center. "Have I told you how much I missed you this
past week?"

"Was that the part about sore eyes?" She could feel
those eyes boring into her profile as she watched the
fire and tried to get control of currents that were
shooting through her at an unholy speed.

"This has never happened to me before—not being
able to concentrate on my work, having my mind wan-
der at the most awkward moments. Something very
strange has come over me, Alexandra."

"Maybe you're allergic," she offered, making light
of it because, as good as it was to hear him say this, it
was also unnerving. Especially when she was so aware
of his muscular thigh pressed against hers.

He traced the upper curve of her ear with his nose.
Then he straightened away from her, but not as far
away as he'd been before. "No sneezing, no itchy eyes,
no rash. You do take my breath away, but I don't think
it has anything to do with an allergy."

Alexandra took a drink of champagne to help swallow back the rapidly increasing wave of desire that was washing through her. "Maybe it's some residual aura from all the time I spent with the snake charmer as a kid."

"Are you calling me a snake?" he asked with a smile in his voice.

"No," she was quick to deny, laughing. "That's not what I meant. I was just making a joke." A joke she'd made with her brain at only half power while the other half was being taken over by her senses—the smell of his after-shave, the sound of his deep voice, the sight of his hair falling just barely to his brow, the feel of his body so close, his arm coming around her now instead of just along the back of the sofa.

"You're the first woman I've ever met who has the power to distract me. Brian says my single-mindedness is what's gotten me where I am. But all of a sudden that single-mindedness has taken a hike, and business has gotten the short end."

Alexandra understood this all too well, because like it or not, fight it or not, the same thing had happened to her since meeting him.

Evan caught the stem of her glass between the same two fingers that bracketed his and leaned forward to set them both on the table. Then he settled back, angling toward her as he did so.

She turned her face up to him and Evan obliged, lowering his mouth to hers, his lips parted. He tasted of the champagne, only better, and Alexandra thought that she'd rather sample it here than from a glass any day, and answered the opening of his mouth with that of hers.

His tongue flicked against the sensitive corners of her mouth, tickling just a little, before delving inside and finding hers. But it was instinct that allowed her tongue to match his because she suddenly became more aware of his arms around her, pulling her against him, his hands slipping underneath her sweater to the bare skin of her back.

Wonderful hands. The man had truly wonderful hands. Big and warm and pressing just firmly enough for her to feel the strength of them without exerting their power.

What would that back of his feel like? she began to wonder. Would it be as hard as it looked? Would it seem as broad beneath his clothes?

Still kissing her, still exploring the recesses of her mouth with his tongue, he edged forward just enough to accommodate her arms as she reached around him and under his sweater to find the answers to her questions.

His bare back was definitely as broad and hard as it looked. Her palms swept over well-honed muscles as they followed the motion of his arms and shoulders.

But again, just as she was getting lost in learning about him he distracted her with his own exploration. Sliding one of his hands to her side, he slipped his thumb into the lace of her bra and followed the rise of it all the way to the front, where he barely touched the outer circle of her nipple with his thumb. But it was enough to send shock waves of pleasure rippling through her, and Alexandra knew what it was to regret not going braless as she ached to feel his hand take her completely.

Maybe it was her slight intake of breath at his touch or the reflexive arch of her spine, but Evan seemed to understand. He made quick work of unhooking her bra and found his way back to do just what her body was crying out for. How could something be soothing and arousing at once? But that first touch of his hand to her nipple was both. She felt it harden in his palm and he responded with a gentle squeeze as his fingers closed around her engorged flesh.

He was wonderfully thorough, giving equal attention to the very crest of her nipple, to the sensitive outer circle of it, to the fullness all the way to her side, to the hollow of her cleavage and then to her other breast— then beginning it all again until Alexandra was breathless.

Just when she was lost in the glorious workings of his hand, in the feel of his fingers teasing, pulling, rolling, gently pinching her nipples, in the texture of his tongue against hers, in the ride of her palms against his naked back, in the desire to give herself over to him fully and completely, the rational half of her brain reasserted itself. She remembered that there was a part of her, of her background, that she couldn't and wouldn't give over to him fully and completely. Common sense cooled her ardor as she remembered how truly complicated her situation was.

She couldn't help the groan of disappointment that rumbled from her throat when she broke away from Evan's kiss and pulled back from his touch. "I don't want this to go too far," she managed to say though a constricted throat that allowed only a whisper.

Evan grimaced and drew a deep, deep breath, as if that was the only way to control what had already been burning inside him, too. He pulled his hand out from under her sweater and clasped the back of her neck in a grip that was just tight enough to convey what an effort it was for him not to finish what they'd started. He dropped his head back and Alexandra saw him swallow hard. Then he sat up straight and opened his eyes.

"Okay," he conceded. "I'd never do anything you didn't want me to."

Wanting had nothing to do with it, but Alexandra kept herself from saying that. Evan exhaled and relaxed, as if his battle for control had been won. Then he wrapped his arms around her again, pulling her so that her cheek rested against his chest.

"Like I said, something very strange is happening to me over you."

"Me, too," she admitted in a small voice that had once more bypassed conscious thought. "But it's a little like a runaway train." She swallowed and pulled back from him again. "I'd better get going."

Evan dropped his arms from around her and, taking her by the shoulders, turned her so that her back was to him. As if he had done it for her a hundred times before, he raised her sweater and refastened her bra, kissing the vertebra just below it, once he had. Then he pulled her sweater down.

"As much as I wish I didn't have to, I'm going to walk you to your car before I lose my head and try some hands-on persuasion to make you stay." He stood and offered her his outstretched hand.

Alexandra took it even though any contact with him was dangerous when she wanted so badly to let what had begun here on this couch reach a satisfying end.

"Tomorrow," Evan said on the way to her car.

"Tomorrow?" she repeated, confused.

"The bigger pieces of the collection are being delivered in the morning. In the afternoon I'm going to take the watches from the safety-deposit boxes they're in now and bring them home. I'd like you to go with me. We can do it just before the bank closes so you can still get a full day's work in, and then have dinner.''

Her internal voice of caution was becoming more and more remote, and this time it was so faint she ignored it. Anyway, she would feel better seeing the Breguet watch safely ensconced in the system she had devised to protect it. ''What time shall I be here?''

''As early as you can make it. If your last appointment is at noon, come then—I'd love to have the whole afternoon to entertain you.''

He was teasing again and it helped to relax some of the sexual frustration Alexandra still felt—but then so did the cold night air as they crossed the courtyard.

''I don't think I can make it before four-thirty.''

He opened her car door and dropped a kiss to her lips. Then he looked directly into her eyes as he said, ''Fine. I'll be waiting.''

Somehow those last words seemed to have two meanings, as if he were telling her he'd wait patiently for her to be ready to finish what they'd started tonight, too.

Alexandra slid into the driver's seat and started her car. ''I'll be here,'' she said brightly, as if she were only thinking of the next day.

Evan closed her door and tapped the hood as if to give her the go-ahead. He was watching her as she turned onto his private road and then she lost sight of him in her rearview mirror; but the imprint of the feel of his hands on her was as vivid in her mind as if he were still with her.

And all she could think was that no matter how unwise it was, she wanted two things: to have more of him, and to give him more of her.

Chapter Six

Tommy and John were having coffee at the kitchen table the next morning when Alexandra finished dressing and went out to begin her day. Her grandfather had water heated for her tea and she made herself a cup. Just as she sat down at the table the phone rang and Tommy did his usual dash into her office to answer it. Alexandra was glad to have a moment alone with her friend.

"Looks like stopping by for your first cup of coffee with Tommy is getting to be a habit this last week or so. I know it's been out of your way a couple of times, but thanks for coming, anyway—he really looks forward to seeing you every morning."

John shrugged. "Hey, I get muffins out of the deal, don't I? Besides, I've been seeing Marissa every night, so that means I need to go straight home after work to shower instead of stopping by here." John's face turned slightly red. "I wasn't getting to see enough of Tommy and I missed him. He's the closest thing I ever came to having a father, too, you know. Anyway, coming by in the morning works better."

Alexandra groaned. "That sort of shoots something I wanted to ask you."

John wrinkled his brow at her and she thought he resembled a big, good-hearted kid. "What?"

"I have an appointment at four-thirty this afternoon that I'd like not to keep. I was going to see if there was any chance of you doing the bid for me."

"Something come up?"

"Evan Daniels is bringing in his collection and he asked me to be there—to make sure the system is functioning right, once he has everything set up. But if you have a date I can postpone the appointment."

"He's bringing all the watches in today, huh?"

"And the clocks and the bigger pieces—they're being delivered this morning. His sister is giving him a housewarming party tomorrow night, so I imagine he wants the collection all in place for that."

"I thought you went to teach him how to run the system last night?"

There was an edge of teasing in John's voice and Alexandra knew he'd seen through her all-business facade. "I did."

John raised his cup all the way to his lips, but before taking a sip he looked over it at her, all innocence. "Is there a problem?"

"No. He has it coded and it's working great."

"But he needs you there today anyway."

Alexandra smiled and narrowed her eyes at her friend. "Do I give you a hard time about your love life?"

"This is love?"

"Personal life. I meant personal life."

John grinned wryly. "Yes, you do give me a hard time about my love life. You have as long as I've known you." He took a bit of muffin and watched his thumb trace the lip of his cup while he chewed it. But in the momentary silence his expression suddenly sobered. He washed his muffin down with a drink of coffee and then looked at her. "You know, sometimes I worry about you."

"About me? Why?"

He shrugged. "Daniels seems okay on the surface, but then so did Curtis the stiff, at first. I just didn't think you'd ever get involved with his kind again."

"*'His kind'*?"

"You know what I mean—a rich guy who looks down his nose at where you come from. At Tommy and his shenanigans."

"I don't think Evan looks down his nose at me. He accepted the carnival stuff. In fact he thought it was great." But she felt very defensive and it came out in her voice.

John obviously hesitated before saying, "And what about the rest? Have you told him that?"

Alexandra had some trouble swallowing her tea. "No."

John nodded. "I didn't think so." His gaze was on his cup again. "It's just that I'd hate to see you hurt like last time."

"I'm not really that involved," she assured him, while a little voice in the back of her mind called her a liar. But she didn't want to hear her own worries put into words. For the moment she wanted to forget them.

"I'll just call the four-thirty appointment and post-pone."

"No, don't do that. I'll get ahold of Marissa and make our date an hour later tonight, so I can do the bid."

"You're sure?"

"I'm sure. It's no big deal." Again he paused. "You be careful, will you?"

"I'm always careful," she said glibly, knowing that it was already too late for that with her feelings for Evan growing a mile a minute. Then she gave John the name and address for the appointment, telling him as much as she knew about what the people were interested in. "I'd better get going," she said as she took her cup to the sink. "I have to meet that salesman about the new line of window sensors. Thanks for changing your plans for me tonight."

John just waved her gratitude away.

"And if you don't bring Marissa around to meet us soon, I'm going to hide out in the back seat of your car the way I did when you took that girl in Wyoming to the drive-in," she threatened over her shoulder as she walked out of the kitchen.

The doorbell rang as Alexandra was crossing the living room. Tommy came out of the office at the same time and headed for it.

"I'm just leaving. I'll see who it is on my way out," she told her grandfather. But Tommy followed her to the door anyway.

Alexandra opened it and stopped short at the sight of the small, spindly man standing on her porch.

"'Lo, Alexandra," he said enthusiastically, grinning so broadly that his already wrinkled face turned into a web of lines and creases.

''Morty,'' she breathed, less in answer to his greeting than in surprise.

Tommy stepped in front of her and opened the screen for his friend. ''Come on in, Morty. Coffee's on and there's warm muffins.''

''How you been, Alexandra?'' Morty asked over his shoulder as he headed for the kitchen

''Fine,'' she answered, turning her head to watch him every step of the way.

''Well, have a good day, darling,'' her grandfather said, turning to follow his friend.

''Tommy.'' She motioned him back with a nod of her head. When he was beside her again she spoke in a very low voice: ''What's *he* doing here?''

''He has a lead on a good used car for me. I don't want to rent any longer than I have to.''

''A used car?'' she repeated suspiciously.

Tommy patted her arm. ''It's okay.''

''I didn't think you were in touch with him anymore.''

''Morty's a friend, darling. Just a harmless old crony. He lives with his daughter and his grandson out in Golden, watches game shows for excitement. Harmless.''

''And this used car?''

''Belongs to a friend of his grandson. It's a sporty little red convertible the boy's mother is taking away from him because he's gotten too many speeding tickets. You know how a teenager is about his car—he's taken such good care of it, it might as well be new.''

''You're sure about all of that?''

''Alexandra,'' Tommy chastised with both his tone and his expression. ''You really do worry too much. The only thing we two geezers are going to do is sit around and trade lies about the old days for a couple of hours before he takes me to see this car. Now, go on to work."

Alexandra looked from her grandfather to the kitchen door, seeing Morty sitting at the table with the coffee and muffin he'd helped himself to, talking to John. He did look like a harmless old man, she had to admit. And he and Tommy had known each other for probably twenty or thirty years. Morty had been retired longer than Tommy had. It was no big deal that they were still friends, she told herself.

"Make sure you see the title on the car," she advised her grandfather.

Tommy just laughed at her. "I will, Alexandra. I will."

"Stay just a little longer, Jeannie. Alexandra will be here any minute and I want you to meet her," Evan told his sister.

"Half an hour more is all I can spare and then I have to get going," she said, stepping out of Evan's way so he could pick up the baby from the bed where Ashley Allyn had just had her diaper and all her clothes changed. "Are you sure you want to hold her again?"

"It's okay. We're both dry now." Evan took the baby back into the living room and sat down with her. "I can't believe how much she's changed since I saw her in the hospital."

"Amazing, isn't it? Kevin says she grows just in the hours he's at work every day."

"Speaking of Kevin and work, did he get a new secretary?"

"Sure. He traded someone downstairs and got a nice older lady with great typing skills. It was just too uncomfortable for him to keep Shelline, knowing that she'd lied to us all. I think Kevin was as upset about her hidden husband as you were. So tell me, how are things with your burglar-alarm lady?''

Evan nuzzled Ashley. ''Alexandra seems so different from any other woman I've met in a long, long time. But she's hard to figure, sometimes.''

''I'm sure she's very nice. But don't let your heart rule your head. You'd better start looking past the surface.''

''What I'd better do is give your daughter her pacifier before these little sounds she's making turn into big cries.''

Jeannie brought him the pacifier and watched while he put it in the baby's mouth. ''I know how much you want a family of your own, Evan. Just don't let it blind you.''

''Who, me?'' he said, playing it cool even though he knew differently. It wasn't that he was blinded by the desire to have what Jeannie and Kevin had, or what Brian and Karla had. The problem here was that his feelings for Alexandra were growing at a faster rate then he could control, and they were hard to see past. But it wasn't something he wanted to tell his sister, so instead he nodded toward the diaper bag. ''Throw me that blanket, Mom. You forgot to wrap this baby up like a papoose again. No wonder she's fussy.''

Evan was just coming out of his house when Alexandra turned off the private road onto the brick drive that curved in front of his courtyard. He was carrying a baby and making faces at it while a woman laughed beside him, reaching the driver's side of a silver station wagon just before he did.

Even without the evidence of the tiny newborn whom Alexandra assumed was his niece, she would have guessed the woman to be Evan's sister, Jeannie. The resemblance was strongest in her eyes and in the identical color of her hair, which was cut in a short, sporty bob. And there was no mistaking the similarity in the way she turned her head, and the way her face looked in laughter.

Just as Alexandra parked behind the other station wagon, the disc jockey on her radio made a teasing comment to his partner about a woman he'd met on a date the previous night as being the "right one." Alexandra's immediate thought was that she'd like to be *the right one* for Evan.

Then she caught herself.

Of all the things she was or would every be, she wasn't that. And she couldn't let herself *want* to be. Any more than she could let herself go back to wanting that fantasy of respectability that had compelled her to marry Curtis. And she wouldn't.

With the baby still in his arms, Evan came to open her car door. "You're late, Dunbar. I've had to hold this poor baby hostage so you could meet the other two most important women in my life."

Meaning she was in that category? Alexandra wondered as she got out of the car. She tried not to let the idea thrill her.

"He's not kidding," the woman standing at the open door of the other station wagon said with a laugh that quirked her mouth exactly the way Evan's did when he grinned. "My brother here has been playing keep-away with my daughter so I couldn't leave before you got here."

Alexandra stole a glance at Evan. He held his niece as close, as naturally, as lovingly as if she were his own child. Alexandra jabbed her chin his way. "Don't let him kid you. Looks to me like he just doesn't want to give that baby back."

Cradling the infant in one arm as easily as a football, Evan draped his other one across Alexandra's shoulders and whispered an aside into her ear: "Shh. Don't help her figure that out."

Perfect picture, Alexandra thought, of Evan holding the baby and her at once. To escape the attraction that image had for her, she stepped out of his reach and held out her hand to the other woman, introducing herself.

"Sorry." Evan apologized for his omission and finished presenting his sister and niece. But that was as far as they got before Ashley Allyn started to cry.

"I have to get her home," Jeannie said, reaching for her daughter.

But even the baby's cries didn't seem to daunt Evan. He went around to the passenger side and leaned inside the car to put his niece into the safety seat, strapping her in securely.

"I hope we have more of a chance to talk tomorrow night at the housewarming," Jeannie said to Alexandra as she got behind the wheel of her car. "I'm glad you're coming."

"I'm looking forward to it," Alexandra told her above the newborn's cries.

Evan locked and closed the passenger door and then came around to do the same for his sister's.

"Mary and I will be here early to make sure everything is set up," Jeannie called through the window. Then she waved goodbye and left.

Evan's arm came back around Alexandra's shoulders as they both watched the car turn onto the private road. When his sister was out of sight he leaned to kiss her ear. "Hello, beautiful," he whispered, making his voice a sexy rumble that sent a little skitter of sparks all through her.

"Sorry I was later than I said I would be on the message I left. I got struck across town in Friday-afternoon traffic."

"We'll still make it to the bank. Let me just grab my keys and lock the house."

They were in his sports car within minutes and as Alexandra settled into the soft leather seat she realized how tense she was. She readjusted her seat belt and tried to concentrate on the fifties music playing on the tape deck as Evan maneuvered into the main stream of cars headed south on Youngsfield.

But nothing helped, and when she caught herself checking out the people in every car around them, watching through the side mirror to see if any of the ones behind were following them, she realized what was going on with her.

Morty.

His reappearance in Tommy's life—especially at the precise time when the Breguet watch was about to be taken from a more unbreachable place—had put her on edge. Then again, she realized that the reappearance of Morty at *any* time was not likely to please her.

She'd never liked him—even as a kid, and without any real reason. Later, when she'd found out what he did for a living, she'd decided her uneasiness about him must have been instinct.

Flashback tension was what she was feeling now, she told herself as they went into the bank. She'd always felt this way about Morty; and now, even when there was no cause, the tension came anyway, like a reflex. That's all it was.

But she still couldn't seem to relax.

The uneasiness stayed with her all the way into the room where she and Evan carried the safety-deposit boxes. It hung on as Evan opened the metal briefcase he'd brought to transport the watches, all the way through his opening four gray bank boxes. In fact, the nearer Evan came to transferring his collection to his briefcase the more tense Alexandra got.

"I've been thinking," she said suddenly. "Maybe you should leave the Breguet here."

Taking the last of the watches from the first box, Evan looked at her curiously. "Why?"

Alexandra shrugged, but it was too stiff to seem nonchalant. "It's just that I know it's special to you because it was the last gift your father gave you, and that kind of sentimental value is irreplaceable."

Evan smiled and began taking watches out of the second safety deposit box. "Are you trying to tell me I shouldn't trust the burglar alarm you sold me?"

"Nothing is as secure as a bank vault."

Evan passed the third box to her. "Are you going to help with these or just stand there while do all the work?" he teased before going on. "I'm confident in your alarm system, Alexandra. What's the use of having the watches if I don't keep them at home? I can't look at them here, I can't enjoy them here. And for me that's the whole point of owning them. The Breguet in particular is one I want with me just because it does have special memories." He leaned over and planted a light, familiar kiss on her tight lips. "But thanks for the concern. And relax."

Easier said than done.

Alexandra's tension didn't get any better on the way back as she again scrutinized all the cars around them. Crossing the courtyard at Evan's house she kept glancing over her shoulder. It seemed that he'd never get the front door unlocked; and once he did and they were in the house, she made sure the dead bolt was in place. On the threshold of the collection room she scanned all the obvious signs of the alarm system to be sure nothing had been disturbed and then hurried to help place the watches on display so she could turn it on.

But when she came across the Breguet she couldn't help slowing down.

Taking the watch from its velvet jeweler's box she held it in her palm. Although it wasn't nearly as remarkable looking as some of the others in the collection, it was very special to Alexandra. After all, it traced back to the roots of her family. It was Tommy's watch.

She ran a thumb along the six notches in the case, remembering how her grandfather had cried when he'd inherited it fourteen years ago, just after her grandmother's death. How proud he'd been when it had come back from the jeweler with that last notch that marked it as his. The watch meant so much to him that holding it in her hand and knowing it didn't belong to him actually made her heart ache.

"You really are stuck on that watch, aren't you?" Evan said, interrupting her study of it.

"I like the simple beauty of it," she replied, not only to cover herself but because it was true. She glanced up to find Evan smiling tenderly at her.

"That's what my father said about it when he gave it to me. That was the reason it appealed to him—why he bought it."

Evan has an attachment to the watch, too, she reminded herself. But still it didn't help much. Tommy's claim to it was more genuine.

"And I'll bet you're still wondering about those notches in the case, aren't you?" he went on. "Maybe I should have its history investigated just to soothe your curiosity."

"No!" She took a breath to recover some aplomb. "I mean, that wasn't what I was thinking about. I was just admiring it."

"Fair enough. When you're finished, put it in that watch dome on the pedestal in the middle of the room. It's my centerpiece."

There really wasn't any sense in holding the Breguet any longer, Alexandra thought. After all, it didn't belong to her family anymore. And it never would again.

She hung it on the hook inside the clear glass dome, held on to the gold knob on the very top and set the dome on the base in the center of the oak pedestal. For a moment she stared at the watch, swaying there inside its crystal cage. It was a beautiful display, she thought. Tommy would approve. And then, with one last look at the heirloom, she went back to hurrying through the placement of the rest of the watches.

"Well, that's it," Evan said about an hour after they'd begun.

He stepped back and Alexandra joined him to look around at the complete collection. "It's very impressive," she said honestly, taking in carved clocks that stood anywhere from a few inches above her head to some that nearly touched the high ceiling, mantel clocks on wall shelves and in curio cabinets, and the display tables arranged around the center pedestal.

Then Evan turned to her. "You've gone pale on me again, Dunbar. Are you all right?"

She tried to smile. "Fine. I'm fine," she assured him a little too brightly. "If everything's where you want it, why don't we turn on the system?"

But he didn't buy that. He clasped the back of her neck and kneaded the knots there. "And you're so tense," he added.

"I'm really okay. I just skipped lunch and I'm a little shaky."

He watched her for another moment and then turned her toward the door. "I have the cure for what ails you, then. Stroganoff, crusty bread and wine. Are you up for it?"

She was up for anything if they could just get out of this collection room and turn on the alarm. "Sounds great."

They went into the living room and closed the double doors behind them. Alexandra turned her back as Evan punched in the code that activated the system.

"All set and the end of business. Now for the pleasure," he growled into her ear as he caught her around the waist and steered them to the kitchen. "Thanks to the marvel of appliances that can be timed to turn themselves on, we can eat."

The small table in the corner of the kitchen was set with a white linen cloth and china plates. If not for the fact that the forks were on the wrong side, Alexandra wouldn't have guessed that Evan had arranged it himself. The fact that he had, and had taken such pains, touched her.

"What can I do?"

He tossed her two hot pads. "You can take the Stroganoff and bread out of the oven. I get anywhere near a hot stove and I'm likely to come out burned beyond recognition."

"I wouldn't want that," she said, teasing him with a slow glance up long jeans-clad legs to the tan chamois-cloth shirt he wore. She was glad she had dressed casually, too—in jeans and a short cream-colored cardigan that was buttoned from top to bottom. She'd debated about leaving on the suit she'd worn for work but at the last minute had made a fast stop at home to change. Had she had more time she would have taken her hair out of the loose Gibson-girl knot at her crown, but since she'd already been late she'd left it.

Evan held her chair out for her when the food and wine were all on the table. Then he lit the candle in the center and turned off the lights. "Ordinarily we could use the dining room but Jeannie already has it set up for the caterers tomorrow."

"I like the hominess of a kitchen," Alexandra replied, watching the golden glow of the candle gild his angular face as he sat down.

Evan picked up his wineglass and held it out for a toast: "To the day the carnival came to town."

Alexandra laughed at that before sipping her wine. As Evan served the Stroganoff she was more interested in him than the food. Who would guess that a mere twenty-four hours apart would leave her this hungry for the sight of him?

That unruly wheat-colored wave had fallen over his forehead, he smelled like mountain air—clean and piney—and Alexandra was vividly aware that her appetite tonight was not for anything edible.

In spite of that, she tasted the beef when Evan did, complimenting him only to hear his confession that the same caterer that was doing his party had provided this meal.

"What is it like growing up in a carnival?" he asked after the initial food chatter.

Alexandra shrugged. "Good and bad, like growing up always is."

"Tell me the good first."

"There was my grandfather—"

"The Great T. C. Dewberry," he supplied with a delighted laugh.

"He was great, too, to me. He still is. Fun and funny and full of energy. Of course he's the most meticulous man in the world, so he lectured me endlessly about cleanliness, but beyond that he was pretty lenient."

"You say that as if he raised you."

"He did. From the time I was six, anyway. My parents were killed in an accident, going from one city to another."

"You said you grew up traveling with the carnival, but I didn't realize that meant you'd lost your parents when you were just a kid. I assumed they were part of it. I'm sorry."

"It would have been worse if I hadn't had Tommy."

"And what about your grandmother?"

"She had a stroke that same year. After that, she had to be in a nursing home. We were in Colorado when it happened and she couldn't be moved, so Denver became our base—where we came back to most often so Tommy could make sure she was getting the care she needed."

"So you moved around all the time? Not just during certain seasons?"

"All the time. We did warm climates in the winter months and cold ones in the summer."

"That must have been tough on you."

"Besides being looked down on, as I told you before, the moving was definitely the hardest part about the carnival. A week, maybe two at the most in any one city, and we'd leave. Every Christmas for as long as I sat on Santa Claus's lap, I asked for a real home." She laughed at the memory.

Evan smiled but seemed to see beyond her amusement to the pain it had caused her. "When did you finally settle down?"

"When I went to college in Boulder. By the time I graduated Tommy was ready to call the traveling quits, too, so he came here and we shared an apartment for about a year before he married Marjorie." She couldn't help the scorn that name put in her voice.

"You didn't like *Marjorie*," Evan repeated with an exaggeration of her tone.

"She was twenty years younger than Tommy, brassy and loud. I could never understand the attraction—except maybe that she was the ultimate cleaning project, because between tons of makeup, the most awful hair, tacky clothes and a house that the health department could have condemned, he had his work cut out for him."

"I take it she was nothing like your debonair grandfather," Evan understated.

"Nothing at all. Anyway, they were married until eight years ago."

"The Great T. C. Dewberry outlived her even though he was twenty years older?"

"Marjorie ran away with the mailman. Tacky right to the end." Alexandra finished her meal. "And there you have my checkered history.'' Or most of it, anyway.

"Except that somewhere in the middle of this, you got married,'' he pointed out.

"Mmm. Just before Marjorie did her disappearing act with the mailman. My wedding was two weeks before Christmas, and the day after New Year's she took off.''

"But you finally managed to get a real home from Santa Claus.''

He seemed to see straight into the center of her; to see the real person she was; to like her, to approve of her, to understand her. It made a swell of warm, powerful emotions wash through Alexandra. "Security and stability. Not the best reasons in the world to get married,'' she admitted. "But Curtis was from a big, close family with roots back to the Pilgrims. The perfect antidote to years of being the unsavory transient.''

"Going into marriage for the wrong reasons—is that why it didn't work out?'' he asked, his tone full of compassion.

She couldn't tell him the truth so she said, "Sort of,'' and changed the subject. "What about you? I've monopolized the conversation long enough. Tell me about your childhood.''

He laughed that laugh she loved. "Boring stuff.'' He pushed his plate away and settled back in his chair, still watching her with those penetrating eyes. "I was born and raised here in Denver. It was an ordinary life—my father was an attorney, my mother a housewife. I took swimming lessons in the summers, played little-league football in the fall. I was a jock all through junior-high and high school, went away to college and lived a wild life with as much emphasis on debauchery as school-work, and here I am.''

"An ordinary life," she repeated, surprising herself with the note of envy that crept into her voice from somewhere far back in her past. Or maybe not so far back, she thought, remembering those renewed longings that had welled up in her when she'd arrived at Evan's to find him holding his niece.

It was clear how closely Evan listened when he again responded as much to how she had said it as to what she had said. "Wanting a real home and an ordinary life so much—I'm surprised you haven't remarried and tried again."

"I learned from my mistakes," she said. "What about you? Didn't you ever get close to marrying?"

"Mmm," he responded, with a nod of his head. "I considered it twice in the last couple of years, actually. And got burned both times."

"What happened?"

"The first time I'd been involved with the woman for nearly a year when she finally said she had something to tell me—she had three kids she'd been hustling off to baby-sitters or making hide in the closet when I came to pick her up. In the *closet* for crying out loud! The kids were great, but the way she'd kept them a secret, treating them that way, soured me pretty thoroughly on Barbara.''

"And the second time?"

"Shelline. I met her eight months ago when I started coming out to look for a house. We spent a lot of time together. She came to New York or we met halfway, and there were enough long-distance calls to keep the phone company blissfully happy. Then, two months ago I was having dinner with her in a restaurant downtown and her husband came up and introduced him-self."

"She was married?"

"Separated. But the point is, she swore she'd never been married before. It was quite a secret to keep." He shook his head. "Being single has probably always been a game of hide-and-seek—we all tend to put our best foot forward and keep our flaws to ourselves un-til the other person happens across them. But I thought three kids and a man who was still legally a husband were things that should have been put up front. Those kinds of secrets—big secrets—and the fact that both women had opted to keep them rather than be honest and open with me, were impossible for me to get past."

Alexandra found it hard to swallow the wine she'd just sipped. Picking up her plate, she took it to the sink while she tried to think of something to say.

But Evan met her there, took her hand and unwit-tingly gave her an escape. "This is not a night we're doing dishes," he informed her, pulling her with him as he went back to the table. He poured more wine into their glasses, handed her hers and then took his own as he maneuvered her into the living room.

"It's raining," Alexandra remarked, catching sight of it through one of the windows that framed the fire-place, and seizing it as a change of subject. She left Evan's grip to take a closer look through the glass. "Rain was the scourge of the carnival, but I loved it. We hauled trailers to live in and a hard rain like this, with sleet mixed in, would pound the tin tops like drums."

Evan joined her at the window, opening it just enough to let in the sound.

"We'll freeze," she said of the cold autumn air that came in with it.

Evan set his glass on the mantel and stood behind her, wrapping his arms around her to pull her back against him. "Better?"

Better than anything in the world, she thought of the feel of his big body enfolding her like a warm cocoon, accommodating her every curve. She managed to reach out from under his embrace to put her glass on the mantel, too, and then hooked her hands around his forearms where they barely brushed her breasts.

"The roads are probably getting slick," she said, thinking that she should leave but having no desire at all to go.

He kissed the top of her head. "But this is so nice."

Which was why she wasn't moving.

They stood there for a while without saying anything, listening to the rain. The residual tension from the afternoon drained out of Alexandra, leaving in its place a wonderful, warm, relaxed sense of how right it was to be there with Evan.

"Do you believe in intuition?" he asked in a low, deep voice that brushed his breath into her hair.

"As in ESP?"

"As in gut feelings that tell you things that don't seem rational or reasonable."

"Like which lottery numbers to pick?"

"Like when you've met the person who's right for you."

Alexandra felt goose bumps erupt on her arms, but a burst of apprehension skittered through her, as well.

"I had the strangest sensation the first time I saw you," he went on. "I can't explain it—it was as if I knew you even though we'd never met. As if something had clicked into place that felt right—that made everything feel right.''

''I know,'' she whispered, because she understood what he meant. She was experiencing it now, in fact; as if their bodies meshed together as no other body might ever fit with either of theirs.

''I'm feeling things for you I thought were only figments of fiction,'' he said. ''Things I didn't think really happened this fast or this strongly, if at all. You've knocked me off my feet, lady.''

He took a deep breath and Alexandra felt his chest expand against her back. She wanted to tell him she felt the same way; but to do that would be to mislead him into thinking they could have more together than they could have. And to say anything else, or to make light of it, would end this moment her heart craved. She couldn't do that, either. So instead, she just let her head rest in the valley of his shoulder, giving physically what she couldn't give verbally.

It seemed to be enough as Evan's arms tightened around her. He nudged her head to the side to kiss her neck, then the soft spot just beneath her jaw. ''I want you, Alexandra. More than I can stand. But if you aren't ready....''

If she wasn't ready? Every nerve in her body had come instantly alive with the first brush of his lips. ''It's a good night to stay off the roads,'' she whispered because it was all the sound she could manage to make.

''Uh-uh,'' he denied. ''Not tonight, Dunbar. Tonight you stay only because you want to, because you want me, not because of extenuating circumstances.'' He moved the neck of her sweater out of the way with his nose and kissed her collarbone, tracing the line of it with his tongue.

She couldn't give herself over to him completely in the sense that she couldn't reveal all the details of her history or risk a commitment to the future, either. But she could give herself to him this way. In fact, she couldn't bear not to.

"I can't go home," she told him, reaching one hand to the back of his head as he worked magic at her earlobe, "because I've never wanted anything in the world more than to stay here tonight with you."

He turned her just enough so that she could see his smile a moment before he lowered his mouth to hers. Then he scooped her up into his arms.

Alexandra had an image of navy blue plaid in the quilt onto which he lowered her, but she was too engrossed in Evan's lips on hers—parted, moist, searing—to care much about anything else.

He lay beside her, with one of his thighs slung over hers, and Alexandra reached all the way around his broad shoulders, learning the rough softness of his chamois-cloth shirt.

There was an urgency in their kiss tonight as mouths opened wide and tongues became more insistent. When Evan unfastened the first button on her sweater, Alexandra pulled back enough to free the way for him to make quick work of it, thinking she might not live long enough to feel his hands on her skin again.

Then she was free of her lacy bra, too, and aching for him.

His hand was just the slightest bit cold when he finally reached her breast and the answering pucker of her nipple only heightened her sensitivity. Nothing had ever felt quite as good as those big, masculine fingers kneading her flesh, tracing the circle of the crest, rolling it, gently pinching and pulling.

Alexandra went to work on the buttons of his shirt, finding her own fingers passion-fumbly and less agile than his. But once she had his shirt off, agility wasn't necessary as she coursed her palms from the base of his rib cage up the widening V to his magnificent pectorals, higher still to his broad shoulders, down to hard biceps and then around to the rippling muscles of his back.

His lips deserted hers and found the hollow of her throat instead. One of his arms lifted her back into an arch that made her breasts stand out as if giving evidence of Alexandra's hunger for the velvety feel of his mouth there. She didn't have long to wait before that hot moistness enveloped the tight tip and his tongue circled it flicking and teasing her.

And then she felt him reach for the waistband of her jeans, slipping his four fingers inside just a scant few inches. This time she arched her back involuntarily, straining against the confines of her own clothes.

Again he couldn't get her out of them fast enough as his hand trailed around to her derriere and he pulled her against his lower half the moment she was bare. But his jeans were the last thing she wanted to come up against; and pulling back, she unfastened the snap on his fly. The zipper was tougher to maneuver, strained as it was from the inside, but she managed.

And then he was naked, too, and this time when he pulled her against him she met warm skin—massive, hairy thighs and the long, hard, thick proof of how much he wanted her.

He shifted just enough so that one of her thighs was between his while his came up between hers, pressing home just enough to heighten her arousal even more as he sucked and nipped and gave her other breast equal time.

Instinct ruled as Alexandra began a natural rhythm against his thigh and Evan matched it pulse for pulse in a preview of what was to come. Then he lowered her flat against the bed again.

She opened her legs for him but misjudged just how big a man he was and had to spread them a little wider as he finally came to her. Slowly, carefully, at first, he only teased her, rolling his hips into hers and then retreating, until Alexandra caught the tightness of his perfect rear end in her hands and squeezed just enough to let him know what she thought of his playful torment.

His responding laugh was a sexy rumble in her ear as he pulled back and made a more effective plunge, entering her only slightly and letting her grow used to the feel of him, to the size of him for a moment, before he eased his way into her completely. That deep penetration set off a scatter shot of sparkling sensations that permeated her whole body.

Then he moved, gently but firmly pushing even deeper, drawing out again, then in. She met the thrusts of his hips until she couldn't keep up, until she was too lost in the explosions erupting inside her, in the growing need he was creating. And then it came—the climax, the culmination. As perfect as the way they fit together. As powerful as the feelings she had for him in spite of herself.

Alexandra wrapped her legs around his. She held him tightly and raised her back from the bed just as she felt the same explosion go off in him. Together they rode with the ecstatic spasms in perfect unison, in matching rhythm, until they'd both gone over the peak.

Slowly, a little at a time, they stopped. Alexandra gave in to the softness of the mattress, savoring Evan's weight on top of her, sliding her palms up his moist back to feel the muscles in his shoulders relaxing at about the same pace hers were.

Evan sighed into her hair and then combed the fingers of both his hands through it to her scalp. "I've been wanting to get ahold of this hair since the day I laid eyes on you. I had fantasies about setting it loose, and then I blew my first chance." He pushed up on his forearms and kissed her. "You okay?"

She couldn't help smiling. "I'm okay."

He kissed her again and then rolled to his back, pulling her with him to lie against his side. Reaching over, he yanked the quilt to cover them both and for a moment they were silent. Then Alexandra glanced at the long narrow window that reached from a few inches above the floor nearly to the ceiling. The drapes were open and white snowflakes drifted to the evergreen bushes just outside.

"The rain turned to snow," Alexandra said as Evan held her closely nestled in his arms beneath the quilt.

"It doesn't matter. I'm not letting you out of here tonight anyway."

Alexandra rested her head on his chest, listening to the strong, steady beat of his heart—and loving him.

That realization struck her like a bolt of lightening.

She loved this man.

Panic rippled through her. When the end of this relationship came it was going to hurt more than the end of her marriage had. How was she going to stand it?

And the longer she spent with him the worse it would be.

She should get up right now and run away as fast and as far as she could go, she told herself. She should never see him again.

But she was blissfully warm and comfortable. She felt as if she were wrapped in a sea of down. She even felt as if she were safe there in his arms; protected.

Maybe she should run for her life. But she just couldn't.

"I'm about to fall asleep, Alexandra," Evan warned in a thick, passion-raspy voice.

"So am I" was all she answered, as if not thinking about anything else would make it go away.

Chapter Seven

Alexandra didn't know what time it was when she woke up the next morning, but she knew it was early. She also knew exactly where she was—wrapped in a huge downy quilt in Evan's arms, right where she'd been when she'd fallen asleep.

She stayed perfectly still, not wanting to wake him, not wanting to disturb such perfect comfort. From the pillow of his chest she could see out the window through the drapes they'd never closed. Bright sunshine reflected off a thin layer of crystalline snow, which sparkled and glistened like thousands of tiny mirrors.

The movement of Evan's hand up her arm made Alexandra shift her gaze to see if he was awake, too. He was, and was looking down at her from eyes that were barely open.

"Good morning," she whispered, wondering if he woke happily, or in a bad mood as Curtis used to.

Evan closed his eyes again and smiled a lazy, silly grin that told her he was different. "It's not a good morning. It's a great one."

"You looked outside?"

"No, I didn't." His other arm came around her and he held her tightly.

"It is a gloriously, gorgeously frosted day."

He turned his head in the direction of the window and squinted his eyes open. "Mmm" was all he said before closing them once again and bringing his chin around to rest on top of her head.

"I love mornings," Alexandra told him. "It made me a fish out of water as a kid, though. Carnival life goes on until late at night, so everybody sleeps until almost noon. I'd have to sneak out the window of the trailer because the door squeaked. And if I dared make a sound even once I was outside, somebody would wake up and complain. John would sneak out, too, and we'd take long walks. It was nice."

Evan didn't say anything, and for a moment she thought he'd gone back to sleep. Then he asked, "How about a horseback ride instead of a walk?"

She lifted her head to look at him. "Are you serious?"

He chuckled, his eyes still closed. "It doesn't take much to please you, does it? Yeah, I'm serious. Then we'll come back and make breakfast. And see what develops...." He trailed off on a lascivious note that left no doubt about what he had in mind.

"Let's hurry so we can get out there before the snow melts." Alexandra only got as far as bracing herself on her elbow before remembering her nudity and the fact that she didn't know the layout of his house. "Is there a bathroom close by?"

"If I say no, does that mean you'll dress here and I can watch?" Still his eyes were shut and he smiled like a contented potentate.

"No. It means I'll do it under the covers."

"Spoilsport." He pointed with his chin in the general direction of a door in the corner. "It's over there. Take as long as you need and wake me when you're finished."

"Will you keep your eyes closed while I get there?"

He opened them to form two navy blue slits. "If you insist."

"I insist."

When he closed his eyes again Alexandra slipped out from under the quilt, grabbed up her clothes and dashed for the doorway.

"Hey, Dunbar?" Evan's voice stopped her just as she was about to slip into the bathroom. "Nice buns."

"Thanks," she called through the door once she was inside, managing to sound blasé. She didn't need to see the grin on his face to know it was there, and she couldn't keep one of her own from appearing in response.

After a quick shower, dressing in her jeans and sweater and using his hairbrush, Alexandra returned to the bedroom. "Coward," she accused when she found him sitting up against the plaid-covered headboard in his robe.

"I was only thinking of you. If you'd rather—" He reached out to untie the belt.

"Never mind." Alexandra stopped him. "Just hurry up so we can go."

"On one condition."

He got off the bed and came to stand directly in front of her. She had brushed out her hair and was pinning it into a loose bun at her crown.

"In my horseback-riding fantasy," he went on, "your hair is loose." He pulled out the pins and the whole mass fell down her back.

"You have horseback-riding fantasies?" she teased him as he cocked his head to one side and ran his fingers through her hair, lifting it, then letting it fall through his hands again.

"Once or twice since meeting you."

"And only of horseback riding?"

"Not quite," he whispered in her ear, flicking the lobe with his tongue. Then he stepped around her, giving her rear end a swat just before he went in to the shower.

The horses greeted them with raised ears and a soft whicker from Livvy when they went into the barn twenty minutes later.

"You guys want a little exercise?" Evan asked the animals, petting first Cotter's nose and then Livvy's.

He led the colt into a separate stall where he gave him fresh water and hay and apologized for leaving him behind. Then he brought two saddles from the tack room, laying one over the half wall that divided Cotter from Livvy as he saddled the mare.

He had put on the same jeans Alexandra had taken him out of the night before, and she feasted on the sight of the tight denim encasing the thighs and derriere she so vividly remembered the feel of. Rather than the chamois-cloth shirt, though, Evan wore a black turtleneck beneath the old leather bomber jacket. His hair was still damp from his shower and he was clean-shaven, smelling of his outdoorsy cologne. But Alexandra had only to dip her nose into the neck of the fleece jacket she'd borrowed from him to get a whiff of that fragrance whenever she wanted it.

When the horses were saddled, Evan led them out of the barn and through the paddock gate. He hung Cotter's reins over the top rail of the fence and went to Livvy's side, motioning Alexandra over with a nod. "Come on, I'll give you a lift up."

She took the offer, holding on to his shoulder with one hand and the horn cap with the other. But once she was in the saddle she couldn't resist raising the hand that had been on his shoulder to push back the wave of damp hair that had once more fallen over his brow.

She met his gaze and smiled at him, thinking that she had never in her life felt what she did for him; feeling a little ashamed to realize that she had married Curtis without experiencing the same depth of emotion.

Evan winked at her, handed her the reins and then took Cotter's from the fence, dragging them over the stallion's head. Alexandra watched him as he swung up into the saddle, appreciating his athletic grace and remembering all too well what it had felt like to have those heavily muscled thighs straddling her. Breakfast and then whatever developed....

Side by side they set off on a path that ran several yards behind the pool house, taking them west past Evan's nearest neighbor and then down to a creek that ran crystal clear and glimmered in the morning sunshine. Snow tipped the few leaves that were still left on the trees and traced the limbs of those branches that were bare like white shadows. Since it was just past seven, no one else was out and the only sounds were the

running water of the brook and the crackle of the
horses' hooves on the frosted ground.

"Something just occurred to me," Evan said after a
while of riding in silence. "The reason the horse you
had as a kid could dance, and roll over and play dead
was because he was part of the carnival, wasn't it?"

"She," Alexandra corrected, loving the sound of his
deep, resonant voice coming to her through the quiet.
"Her name was Bridget."

"And there was only one?"

"Only one full-size horse. We had four Shetland
ponies we sold rides on, but they got such a workout by
the paying customers that we had to leave them alone
when they weren't working."

"What else did you have?"

"There were several amusement-park rides—the
biggest draws were the Ferris wheel and a carousel with
hand-carved horses that were Tommy's pride and joy.
Then, we had shooting galleries and shell games and
baseball tosses. The usual."

"Any acts besides your grandfather's imitation of
Houdini?"

"Tommy was the main attraction, but we had a jug-
gler and a magician, a sword swallower, a fire-eater, a
knife thrower, a bearded lady, a fortune-teller, and a fat
lady—John's mother was the fat lady. She thought it
was great to make money by sitting in a chair and letting people look at her. She'd say there was no better
job in the world, especially since it gave her an excuse
to eat everything in sight. When Tommy sold the carnival she went to a spa and lost three hundred and seventeen pounds. Now she's an aerobics instructor in
California."

Evan laughed. "And the bearded lady—did she really have a beard?"

"Absolutely. Three of them that hung in a velvet-lined box on the wall of her trailer every night after her show."

"Smart aleck."

"Well, they were hers. She owned them free and clear."

"And what did you do?"

"A little of everything. Grooming the animals, feeding them and cleaning up after them. Selling admission tickets, running the booths if someone was sick or when they wanted a break, selling hot dogs and popcorn and cotton candy. Stuff like that."

"But you didn't perform?"

Alexandra laughed. "As I got older Tommy wanted me to join his act, but I was more comfortable doing the bookkeeping."

"And John?"

"As a kid he did the same things I did. When he got older he went to work doing most of the maintenance on the rides and the truck engines. He was always very mechanically inclined."

"He didn't want to do time as the fat man alongside his mother?"

"John couldn't have even if he'd wanted to. No matter how much he eats he never gains a pound."

"And his father? Was he part of the carnival, too?"

"Noo. Even talking about his father was off-limits. Seems Mom and Dad weren't married, and Dad wasn't inclined toward it—baby or no. John never knew him."

There was something too charged with energy in the bracing morning for them to keep the slow pace. Or maybe it was the energy Alexandra felt as a result of spending time with Evan. But either way, she was itching for a gallop across the open field that stretched to the north of the creek.

"So, Daniels," she said with challenge in her voice. "Do you really know how to ride that horse?"

Evan's answering smile was slow and cocky. "Are you looking for a race?"

"Could be."

"Stakes," he demanded.

"Loser cooks breakfast and cleans the mess while winner sits on her duff."

"Or on *his* duff."

She gave him a single-sided smile that matched him, cockiness for cockiness. "Deal?"

"Deal."

Alexandra pointed to a stand of trees in the distance. "There and back to the path," she said. And then, without waiting for him to agree or to set a starting time, she put her heels to Livvy's flanks and bolted off the dirt trail into the lead.

There were still shards of ice crystals in the air and Alexandra felt them against her cheeks as she leaned over the horse's neck to gain speed. Livvy must have been feeling the same urge, because with a free rein the animal ran as if she didn't have a rider.

Reaching the trees, Alexandra rounded a cottonwood, with Evan close behind, an expression of pure devilishness on his face that told her he'd been holding back. Until now.

He overtook her with ease and an ornery smile, but Alexandra didn't mind. As she let Livvy do the work, she kept her eyes on Evan and the masculine beauty of his horsemanship. He leaned his head and shoulders into the ride, while the cold air swept back his wheat-colored hair and burnished red the skin above his coat collar. That disreputable leather jacket billowed out behind him, rising enough to provide a glimpse of his attractive derriere and his powerful thighs bulged against the animal's sides. A beautiful beast and a magnificent man. Cooking breakfast was a small price to pay for this view.

"I'll have my bacon crisp but not burned, my eggs over easy, my toast light with butter and jam, and my coffee hot and black" was how he greeted Alexandra when she reached the path only moments after he did.

"You're a hustler," she accused with mock indignation as they let the animals walk home to cool off. "You held back until Livvy was pooped and then pushed Cotter on the last lap."

"That's called racing strategy. I'll also have orange juice—fresh squeezed."

Just what she'd like to be.

Back in the barn Evan unsaddled the animals, brushed them down quickly, fed them and then caught Alexandra around the waist to guide her to the house. But once in the kitchen, coats discarded, Evan pulled her into his arms rather than answering her question about where the frying pan was.

He filled both of his hands with her loose hair and cupped the back of her head. "Fantasy fulfilled. One of them, anyway. Now I'm having another."

"I know. Bacon, eggs, toast, juice and coffee."

"Not quite," he said in a low, sexy voice.

When his mouth reached hers it was open. He thrust his tongue inside and Alexandra welcomed it with her own. The energy-charged morning air had left her feeling alive and carefree. With one touch from Evan, all that was channeled into an instant, pressing need for more from him than a horse race.

His hands went up the back of her sweater and he groaned approval when he found she'd left her bra off. Let him think it was a sensual act of deliberate omission, she thought, when in reality she just hadn't been able to find the undergarment.

He kneaded her sides just once before pressing his way around to her front to take one breast fully in each hand. Freshly squeezed. Alexandra couldn't help the moan of pleasure that rolled from her throat.

Slowly he ended the kiss that was by now wide mouthed and erotic. "I think," he said, dipping back again to pull her upper lip between his, "that we need to reverse the order of our plans—" he gave her another kiss "—and save breakfast for later." He raised her sweater and bent to circle one of her nipples with the tip of his tongue.

Alexandra dropped her head back and felt a ripple of pleasure swirl through her. "Good idea," she managed in a raspy voice.

For a moment he took the crest of her breast fully into his mouth, drawing it deep, flicking it with his tongue and then abandoning it to do the same with the other. Air-drying moisture turned both nipples into tight points of desire when he rose away from his work there and cupped her rear end in both hands. That was all he needed to lift her—as if she weighed nothing— and carry her the few feet to the table where he set her on its oak top. Then he slid his hands along the undersides of her thighs, raising her legs to wrap around him as he pushed the hard bulge of his zipper against her.

Again his mouth and tongue found hers in a forceful dance as he unfastened the buttons of her sweater and spread it to free her breasts to his hands once more.

Alexandra's palms ached for the same feel of him and she pulled his turtleneck from the waistband of his jeans. Reveling in her newfound familiarity with his body, she again took her fill of his broad shoulders, hard pectorals, even his tightened male nubs, before instinct and desire forced her to smooth her hands down his rib cage over his tight belly and then below his waistband to where the tips of her fingers met the tip of his passion.

"Oh, yes," he breathed husky encouragement in a passion ragged voice.

His snap popped and the zipper opened on its own against the strain of Alexandra's hand over his long, thick flesh. Hot, hard and silky and magnificent—ah, yes, he was magnificent everywhere.

Evan's jaw dropped, his head fell back and Alexandra watched what she could do to him....

And then need accelerated everything. He slipped her sweater off and shucked his turtleneck. Next went her jeans and underwear all in one sweep, and then his.

"On the kitchen table?" she asked, sounding more scandalized than she'd meant to.

It made Evan laugh. "There's a first time for everything."

"How—?" But his mouth at her breast cut her curiosity short and from there she forgot to pay attention to the mechanics and lost herself in sensation. Somehow he was inside her and doing all the right things at the right moments with his hands, his fingers, his mouth, his tongue, his body, until explosions—white-hot and wonderful—went off in Alexandra. Again and again, ecstasy surged through her as Evan plunged deep and finally erupted at what felt like the very center of her body.

For a moment they were perfectly still. Then Evan chuckled just a little in her ear. "Definitely on the kitchen table."

"Mmm," Alexandra agreed in a contented groan.

And then the phone rang.

Maybe the peak she'd reached in lovemaking had heightened her sixth sense along with the other five, but somehow Alexandra knew the call was for her.

"We have to answer that," she said.

Evan looked down at her, frowning curiously. "Did you sub for the fortune-teller, too?" he asked, leaving her to pick up the phone.

But Alexandra didn't answer him. Instead she pulled on her clothes as if the house were on fire.

"I guess this shouldn't come as a surprise, but it's for you," he said, holding out the receiver and looking at her as if she'd just done a magic trick he couldn't figure out.

Buttoning her sweater as she crossed the kitchen, Alexandra took the phone from him, knowing something was wrong the same way she'd known the call was for her.

"Sorry to bother you," John apologized sheepishly on the other end of the line. "But the police are here questioning Tommy and I think you'd better come home fast."

"I'll be there in fifteen minutes." She hung up and headed for the living room. "I have to go home."

Evan had dressed while she was on the phone. He tucked his shirt in as he followed her. "What happened? Is it your grandfather?"

"Sort of" was all she would say as she grabbed her purse from the chair where she'd left it the night before.

"I'll drive," Evan said.

"No!" Tension made her tone harsh. Alexandra amended it. "Just stay here. Tommy is all right. There's just a problem and I have to go." Which was what she did, rushing out of the house without another word.

It wasn't until she turned onto Youngsfield that she realized Evan was a few cars behind hers, dodging in and out of traffic to catch up.

"Damn!" she muttered to herself. Then, to the rearview mirror image of his sports car as it slipped in directly behind her she said, "Go back. Go home."

But the jig was up and she knew it.

There was only one police car in front of her house—a good sign, she thought as she ran across her front lawn without waiting for Evan.

It was Tommy who greeted her as she rushed into the house. He was standing in the middle of the living room dressed in his maroon brocade dressing gown, in front of two policemen. "Alexandra! Tell these men that I would never leave a mess. Imagine anyone thinking I might be connected with a job where the house was trashed? I can't believe it."

"Hold on, Tommy," she said to calm her grandfather. Evan came in just then, but Alexandra had more pressing things to deal with and didn't spare him more than a glance. Instead she turned to the officers. "What's the problem?" Then belatedly she added, "I'm his granddaughter."

"There was a robbery last night is what happened," Tommy explained before either of the two policemen could get a word out. "And since I'm the most recently released convicted thief out of the state penitentiary, I was understandably first on the dance card of suspects. Except that I shouldn't have even made the list, given that the house was vandalized in the process." He pointed to the plate-glass window and addressed one of the officers again. "Look at that. Do you see so much as a speck on it? Spotless. And I keep it that way. Had the owners come home to find their windows washed for them, you would have reason to suspect me. But not as it is."

Leave it to Tommy to be more incensed over being blamed for a mess than for a burglary. Alexandra looked to one of the policemen for confirmation. "Then this is just routine?"

"We needed to know where your grandfather was between the hours of midnight and three this morning," one of the uniformed men finally offered.

Of all the times for her not to have slept at home.

Just then, John came in from the kitchen, his shirt wrinkled and untucked, his hair uncombed. He handed one of the officers a sheet of paper. "Those are the names and addresses of the other guys," he said.

"My alibis," Tommy informed Alexandra.

John filled in with an explanation her grandfather seemed too affronted to give. "We played poker here last night. Everybody else left around four and I slept on the couch."

Alexandra looked at the policemen. "Does that put my grandfather in the clear?"

"So long as there's corroboration, I can't see that there'll be any problem." The officer had some trouble suppressing a smile as Tommy swiped a white handkerchief along the mantel and insisted that the other policeman see the proof that it was completely dust-free. "We'll be in touch if we have any other questions."

The police left and John pushed a weary hand though his hair. "Make me some coffee, will you, Tommy? If I don't get a shot of caffeine I don't think I can stay awake to drive home."

Looking more alert than the younger man, Tommy glanced from Alexandra to Evan and back again. "Can I do anything for you two?"

Alexandra shook her head, suddenly realizing that there was no way to avoid a lot of explaining to Evan. Time to face the music. She turned to him and tried a smile that didn't fit. "Can we talk outside?"

He was looking at her as if he didn't know her, but he opened the door and waited for her to go out. Alexandra did, and sat down on the front-porch glider whose cushions she had yet to put away for the winter.

It was a bit of a blow to her that Evan didn't join her there. Instead he went to the wrought-iron railing. Leaning back against it, he crossed his arms over his chest and stared at her. "Your grandfather is a convicted thief?"

His tone was calm. There was no condemnation in it—yet. Alexandra took a deep breath. "A carnival isn't the most profitable endeavor in the world, even for the owner. Tommy made enough to survive, but not much more. When my parents were killed in the accident, my grandfather didn't only suffer the loss personally. There was also the blow of losing two of the carnival's integral people along with the truck and all the equipment it was carrying. Even with insurance it was a financial catastrophe that nearly sank him professionally. Through loans Tommy managed to stay afloat, but then my grandmother had her stroke.''

Alexandra paused a moment as it struck her how quietly, how intently, Evan was listening, never taking his eyes off her. Curtis had paced his way through this story, flinging his arms up in horror at the revelation of her background, saying *I can't believe it!* every two minutes, his disgust echoing off the walls. Was it a good sign that Evan's reaction was more patient? Or was he just thinking that now was the time the skeleton in her closet got revealed to sour him in the same way learning those other two women's secrets had?

She went on. "Tommy loved Rose. Sometimes I wonder if people today even know how to love someone the way he did. The stroke left her in a vegetative state—that was the technical term—and seeing her like that nearly killed him. Even as young as I was, I can remember how hard it was for him. He looked awful, he didn't sleep, his eyes were always bloodshot, he wouldn't leave the hospital for days at a time.''

"What about you? Who took care of you?''

"I stayed with John and his mother.''

"It must have scared the hell out of you—a six-year-old kid losing both of your parents and your grandmother in the space of a couple of months.''

"Maybe that's why I remember it all so vividly. I was pretty scared,'' she admitted, finding another difference between Evan's response and what her former husband's had been; Evan showed concern for her, while Curtis had worried about his family's reputation. But she tried not to let her hopes get too high.

"If not for John and his mom I probably would have had more scars, but they were like family and I knew I was loved. It helped. Anyway, when it became clear

that my grandmother would live but never re-
gain ... anything, the hospital recommended a nursing
home. Tommy wouldn't hear of it. He said he'd take
care of her." Alexandra shook her head at the memory. "He tried, too, bless his heart. But there was just
no way. She had to have professional care and that was
all there was to it. When he finally admitted it to himself he started visiting nursing homes. He'd come back
fighting mad at the conditions—Tommy was always
very meticulous, but some of what he said he saw
would have revolted anybody. There was no way *his*
Rose was going in a place like that, he said. Then he
finally found one he could stand putting her in. Trouble was, it was private and expensive and the govern-
ment aid he received to help with the cost of
grandmother's care didn't make a dent."

"So he became a thief?"

Alexandra sat up a little taller. "He tried selling the
carnival but he couldn't make more than what he
needed to cover the loans from the accident. Full-time
locksmithing didn't provide what he needed, and even
keeping the carnival going and locksmithing on the side
weren't enough. There were only two choices—see my
grandmother put in a shabby home, where she'd have
minimal, understaffed attention, or put his combined
knowledge of locks and escapes to work for him."

"So he became a thief," Evan repeated.

"In his day he could pick any lock and figure out
how to bypass any security system, and then on his way
out he'd reset them so no one could come in after him
to do something he wouldn't have done—that's why he
was so upset with the police for accusing him of burglary where there was vandalism. He took pride in not
doing *that*, at least, to the people he robbed." It

sounded like feeble compensation even to her. "I'm not saying what he did was right. It wasn't. And I know not leaving a mess doesn't make a burglary any more acceptable, but he did do it out of necessity."

"You grew up with this?"

She shook her head. "I didn't know about it as a kid. In fact I didn't find out any of this until eight years ago. I always just thought he paid the bills like everyone else—even when I got older and handled the books for the carnival. I knew how marginal the profits were, but he said he had the money for my grandmother's care put away, and he handled that. Maybe I was gullible, but it never occurred to me that he was stealing it."

"How long did the burglaries go on before he got caught?"

Alexandra picked her words carefully, wishing she didn't have to tell him the whole story. "He didn't get caught for the robberies that supported my grandmother. She lived for fourteen years after her stroke and in all that time he never got so much as a parking ticket." She saw a flash of something cross Evan's face but she couldn't tell what emotion it was. She looked away.

"Then, how is it that he just got out of jail as a convicted thief?" Evan asked when she didn't go on.

"Marjorie."

"Marjorie?"

"When Rose died, Tommy stopped stealing." Alexandra paused. She could lie here, she offered herself. But she didn't want to. And she realized suddenly that somewhere deep inside she had a fantasy of her own—that a man would know the truth about her background, about Tommy, and love her in spite of it. Love her the way Tommy had loved Rose.

She raised her chin a little and went on. "Ironically, a few months after my grandmother died Tommy inherited a family heirloom worth a lot of money. It meant a lot to him. He was so proud of his legacy...." She trailed off, thinking about that for a moment before catching herself. "Anyway, then Tommy married Marjorie. When she decided to run away with the mailman she took Tommy's inheritance and sold it. He was more upset about that than about her leaving. He tried to buy the heirloom back with the money he'd made from finally selling the carnival after all those years—money Marjorie couldn't get her hands on because it was in a bank account under Tommy's name alone—but he didn't have enough and the buyer wouldn't bargain. Tommy could hardly go to the police, so even though he'd stopped stealing he opted for one last burglary to get back what was his. Only he hadn't kept up on the new alarm systems. He got caught. It took a little over eleven months to go through the legal process, but he was convicted and has been in jail for the past seven years."

"You didn't say what the heirloom was."

Alexandra looked Evan straight in the eye. "It was the Breguet watch your father gave you. He must have bought it from Wizencrantz—the man Marjorie sold it to."

Alexandra saw the shock on Evan's face and had the urge to go on talking, to say anything rather than look at that expression. "I know, it's quite a coincidence. For a minute, when I first saw that the watch was a part of your collection, I was a little worried. That's why I asked how you'd heard of Security Systems. But then

Brian said he'd seen the interview. During Tommy's trial a reporter dug up enough of his past to learn that he'd been under suspicion for a number of earlier robberies. Tommy all but admitted to the ones where the statute of limitations had expired, offering details about resetting alarms and sometimes washing the dishes before he left or leaving a pair of shoes polished. The article made it to a national magazine and for a while he enjoyed a little notoriety—he calls it his fifteen minutes of fame. Anyway, as I told you, he thinks a connection between a successful burglar and Security Systems would be a great angle. Sort of what you thought when you found out he was an escape artist. I'm pretty sure he suggested me for that interview, because the host asked about my relationship with Tommy. I changed the subject fast, but when I heard that Brian had seen the program I realized that you guys didn't know anything about Tommy or his connection with the watch, and since you hadn't picked my company because of some anonymous soliciting, the whole thing had to be a coincidence."

She was rambling and she knew it. She stole a glance at Evan. He was frowning and she had the feeling it wasn't at anything she'd said.

"And Tommy's been in the state penitentiary in Canon City for the past seven years?"

He was obviously putting two and two together. Alexandra didn't answer him.

"He wrote the letter making the offer for the watch, didn't he?" Evan asked.

"I don't know. I don't even know if he has any idea that you own the watch. I don't think he does and I don't think he wrote the letter, because since meeting you that first night we went out he hasn't asked a thing he wouldn't ask about any man I know. If it was Tommy who made that offer on the Breguet, certainly he'd have been in touch with you or at least said something to me about why you haven't answered.''

"But you haven't asked."

"Directly? No. I don't want to stir anything up. He talks about the watch a lot. I think maybe he just told someone else about it—someone who lives in Canon City and is a collector himself or just a watch lover— and they tracked it to you."

"If you really believed that, why did you want to upgrade the system the day after I told you about the letter? And why did you want me to leave the Breguet in the bank? Why were you so nervous about taking it out?"

"Tommy will never steal anything again," she said forcefully rather than answer his questions. "Do you know what his time in prison did to his dignity? It isn't something he would ever chance having happen again."

"But just in case, you installed a more complicated system so if he was thinking about reclaiming the watch he'd be discouraged."

There was no denying the truth of what he suggested, so Alexandra didn't try. Instead she just stared at him, seeing his doubts and suspicions as clearly as she'd seen them in other people all her life. As clearly as she'd seen them in Curtis.

"In case you're wondering," she said ruefully, "I've never stolen a thing in my life."

Evan gave a humorless little chuckle at that and pushed off the railing. He came to sit beside her the way she wished he would have before, taking her hands in his and looking at them, his expression sober. "Yes, you have. I think you've stolen my heart. I'm falling in love with you, Alexandra.''

If there was ever a stranger time to be told such a thing, she couldn't imagine it. Not that it mattered. In fact it was a strangely wonderful time for him to say it—just when she was sure he was about to reject her the way Curtis had.

"I think I'm falling in love with you, too," she whispered, wondering if, just maybe, this time love might be a strong enough antidote to her background.

He kissed her then—a soft, warm kiss that didn't seem any different from any other kiss he'd given her yet. Did that mean things between them could go on as they had been? Unharmed by any of what she'd revealed?

"I know you wouldn't steal anything," he said then, giving her hope. "I have to go home. Jeannie and the people she's hired for the party will be wandering in any time this morning. Can I come and pick you up tonight?"

Alexandra had forgotten his housewarming. Again it seemed like a good sign to her that he hadn't; that what she'd told him hadn't taken precedence over everything else. "Picking me up would be a waste of gas. Just stay and get ready for your party and I'll drive over myself."

"You don't mind?"

Such a small thing in view of so many bigger things that might have done so much more damage. "I don't mind."

"Then I'll see you tonight."

He kissed her once more, winked at her and left. But once he was gone, Alexandra's buoyant spirits took a dive.

Evan hadn't said one word about Tommy or what she'd confided. So she didn't have any idea what he might be thinking about her grandfather.

Chapter Eight

It was still early when Evan finished dressing for the party that evening. Not wanting to get in the way of the caterer or the serving people Jeannie had hired, he went to the pool house. Brian called for him to come in when he knocked and Evan found his friend in the bathroom, shirtless, and his face covered with foam as he began to shave.

"Fix us a drink, why don't you?" Brian said by way of greeting.

"Scotch on the rocks?"

"A light one. I have to pick up Karla."

Evan found the liquor in a cupboard over the stove and brought two glasses of ice and amber liquid back to the bathroom. Handing Brian one, he took a sip of the other and leaned a shoulder against the door. "Ever heard of T. C. Dewberry?"

Brian frowned into the mirror. "Sounds familiar.... Wait a minute, isn't that who you said Alexandra's grandfather is—The Great T. C. Dewberry?"

And apparently he was great at more than just an escape-artist act, Evan thought. "I forgot I told you. Had you ever heard of him before that?"

"Why would I have heard of him before that?"

"His name was mentioned in that interview you saw of Alexandra."

"Was it? Hell, I don't remember. I was packing up my stereo for the guy I sold it to when that show was on. The TV was just background noise. I wasn't paying that much attention."

"And you don't remember ever hearing of him before, either?"

"No." Brian stopped shaving, took a drink of his Scotch and looked at Evan. "Why? Should I have?"

It was Evan's turn to frown. "Seems as though he was a pretty notorious thief several years ago."

Brian's mouth dropped open. "Alexandra's grandfather is a card-carrying thief?"

Evan told him the whole story. When he'd finished, Brian went back to shaving, but his actions were all very deliberate.

"What are you thinking?" Evan asked.

Brian shook his head, obviously reluctant to say. "I know you have some feelings for this woman," he soft-pedaled.

"I think I'm in love with her."

Brian rinsed suds off his razor, letting the water wash over it for longer than he needed to, clearly buying himself time to gauge his words. "Then maybe you have a better idea of what's going on than I do and I should keep my mouth shut."

"Say what's on your mind."

He didn't for a few minutes, sipping his drink. Then he said, "I'm just wondering how safe it is to have a thief's granddaughter put in a security system. That could be quite a racket—she gets hired by people with something to protect, installs the burglar alarm and then gives her grandfather all the information he needs to break into it."

Evan threw back a mouthful of Scotch and pushed away from the doorjamb to pace the hall.

"You did say you wanted to know what was on my mind," Brian reminded.

"I meant it," Evan grumbled.

"Shall I go on?"

"Yes."

"Even if Security Systems isn't some burglary ring—"

"It isn't."

"Okay. But even if it isn't, I think we need to consider some things that make you a target. Namely that you own the heirloom watch that was the old man's most prized possession. The same watch that someone else stole from him, that he went to jail for trying to steal back once. Even if his granddaughter isn't in on it, her company just installed the burglar alarm that's supposed to protect the watch. That makes her plans for the layout pretty accessible, not to mention the information on the workings of the system. And with you involved with Alexandra, her grandfather also has knowledge of the kind of hours you keep and when you're out of the house. And..."

"Go on, you haven't hit on anything about her grandfather that I haven't already thought of," Evan prompted when his friend stalled.

"Yeah, but this is the part you don't want to think about. Going back to square one—if Alexandra and Security Systems is on the up-and-up, wouldn't she have refused to take this job the minute she saw the watch?"

"I'm sure she had her reasons in spite of the watch." Evan didn't hesitate to defend Alexandra.

"Let's just hope they were reasons other than getting her grandfather's inheritance back."

"I don't believe Alexandra is dishonest or in on any plot to get the watch back," he said, unable to keep a sharp note out of his voice.

"See. I shouldn't have said anything. If our positions were reversed and you were saying things like this about Karla, I'd want to punch you, too."

Evan shook his head. "I'm sorry. I asked for it." He took another pull of Scotch and a deep breath to calm himself down. He didn't want any more of the thoughts he'd been having all day long. Thoughts that reminded him that Alexandra hadn't wanted him to pick her up for their first date or been anxious for him to go into her house anytime—sure signs of hiding something. He didn't want to wonder if she would eventually have offered the information about her carnival background if he hadn't run into her grandfather. He didn't want to wonder if she eventually would have told him about Tommy's past and the watch. But none of it had anything to do with his friend.

Brian finished shaving, patted his face dry and ventured carefully, "Maybe we should have someone from a different security company come in and check out the system—like a second opinion from a doctor—just to make sure it's doing the job it's supposed to."

Evan was tempted, he had to admit. He hated himself for it, but he was tempted nonetheless.

Brian went from the bathroom to the bedroom. "Will you be able to rest otherwise?"

"I care for this woman," Evan said, rather than answer Brian's question directly.

"Could be you'll find out she did one hell of a job and put in an alarm that no one can beat. Then you can relax."

Evan wandered into the living room. In spite of all his wondering today, he'd realized that his feelings for Alexandra weren't like anything he'd ever had for any other woman. This had to be love because it was so powerful, so intense.

"I don't think we need to have the system checked out," he finally decided.

"What harm would it do?"

That was a good point. Then again, the harm might be in knowing he hadn't trusted Alexandra. And even if only he and Brian knew it, that lack of faith might do insidious damage to the way he thought of her. He had to trust her. "Let's just let it ride for now."

Brian came out of the bedroom buttoning his shirt. "If you find out the system is great you'll know you don't have anything to worry about. If you find out it isn't... Well, isn't it better to know before something happens? Before you're in any deeper with her than you already are?"

"I can't be in any deeper than I already am," Evan said, more to himself than to his friend. Then he looked Brian in the eye. "Trust is something you have until it's proven otherwise, not something you only have after you've looked under every rock for a reason not to have it."

"And you trust her?"

"I don't believe she'd do anything wrong," he answered without hesitation, meaning it. "That's not to say that I don't have some qualms about her grandfather."

"Then we should have the system looked at and maybe changed or expanded just enough to prevent the old man from knowing exactly what's up our sleeves."

Evan shook his head. "I'm betting that she's gone out of her way to install a Tommy-proof system already."

"Losing that bet could be pretty expensive for you."

Hashing this out aloud had cleared some of Evan's doubts. Maybe he'd just needed to blow off some steam, because he suddenly realized that he believed what he was saying. "I'll put my money on Alexandra." Then he changed the subject. "How about you? How are things on the financial front?"

"Don't ask."

"That bad?"

"That bad." Brian looked at the clock on the wall above the mantel. "I have to get out of here and pick up Karla or we'll be late for this shindig of yours tonight."

"I'll get out of here, then." Evan put his glass in the sink and went to the front door, but before he left he couldn't resist saying, "You know I'm here if you need me."

"I know. Thanks." Brian paused a moment, then added, "The same goes for you."

"Oh, for crying out loud!" Alexandra complained when her hand jerked for the third time and smeared nail polish up her finger. She wiped it off with a little remover and took a deep breath. Why was she so jittery tonight?

"That's a stupid question," she muttered to herself.

She'd spent the whole day getting ready for this party and wondering if this morning's revelations were the beginning of the end for her relationship with Evan. And worse, if it *should* be—if she should bow out now before she got hurt.

But the conclusion she'd come to was that she cared so much about him already that, either now or later, ending their relationship would hurt. So she might as well ride it through to the finish, she'd decided, trying hard not to hope that maybe there wouldn't have to be an end—that just maybe things would work out with Evan; that maybe he was the Tommy in her life who would love her in spite of everything, the way her grandfather had loved her grandmother.

"Big night planned?"

Alexandra jumped and this time the nail polish hit the newspaper that protected the kitchen tabletop.

"Sorry," John apologized, sitting across from her. "I didn't mean to scare you."

"It's okay." Alexandra finished her last nail and sat back to look at her friend. "No date tonight?"

"Marissa went to Phoenix for the weekend to visit her parents."

Alexandra nodded. "I see. That's why you played poker last night. And thank goodness you did. I don't know what I'd have done if Tommy hadn't had those alibis."

John glanced at her pale pink fingernails. "Where are you headed tonight?"

"Evan's housewarming party."

Both of John's eyebrows arched high on his forehead. "Even after this morning?"

Alexandra nodded. "And I told him the whole story, too." She laughed at herself. "Boy, that sounded confident, didn't it? As if I were glad I did because now everything was out in the open and worked out great."

"It isn't the way?"

She shrugged. "He didn't run screaming into the night. But I can't help wondering how things will change between us, now that he knows."

"Maybe they won't."

"Yeah, maybe."

"How did he take it?"

"I don't know. He didn't say a word about it. Just told me he loved me."

John's eyebrows went up even higher. "That's good, isn't it?"

"I guess so. I just can't help thinking that maybe it was a cover-up for his feelings about the other stuff. That not addressing Tommy's past in any way was an ominous omission."

"You're thinking of Curtis, aren't you? If this guy accepted the carnival stuff better than Curtis did, maybe he's just taking Tommy's criminal record in stride, too."

Alexandra laughed ruefully. "Maybe," she allowed. "Lord knows, Curtis didn't keep his disapproval quiet. Remember just after I told him about the carnival and he wanted me to disinvite Tommy from his parents' Christmas party?"

"I remember that the night of the party was a long one."

"Just you and me and Tommy watching television."

"With Tommy wondering where Marjorie was since she hadn't come home in two days, and you crying all the way through a slapstick comedy."

"And Tommy trying to find out what I'd fought with Curtis over that had kept us both from going to the party. I guess in a way I was lucky the marriage didn't last. I couldn't have gone through the rest of Tommy's life telling him I'd had a fight with my husband, to keep us both from going to every party Curtis or his family ever had. And I could never have told Tommy the truth."

"Curtis was a creep," John said loyally.

"A first-class one," Alexandra agreed.

"And you think this guy is different?"

"I don't know for sure, but I think so. I hope so."

"I hope so, too." John stood and pushed his chair in. "Well, I'd better go downstairs and see if I can speed up Tommy's dressing or we'll miss the budget price on the movie tonight. You think you'll, uh, be coming home? Or should I sleep on the couch just in case Tommy needs another witness?"

Alexandra felt heat rise in her cheeks. "I'll be home after the party. You don't have to stay."

"I don't mind."

"Thanks, but I'm coming home. Early."

John shrugged. "Okay."

He left and Alexandra gathered up her nail gear and headed for the bedroom in a hurry. She'd washed and curled her hair, catching it up high on the crown of her head and letting it cascade down her back in a riot of spirals. With her makeup finished, she had only to slip on the cowl-necked tunic waiting on her bed and the black skirt that fell to midcalf. Once the skirt was fastened, she belted the tunic low over her hips and then pulled on tall, high-heeled black boots.

She made one last check in the mirror, aware that her heartbeat had kicked up a notch at the thought that within minutes she'd be back with Evan.

Would he have a different attitude toward her? she couldn't help wondering. Or was it possible that nothing would change between them?

Her palms were damp and she smoothed them down her skirt, squaring her shoulders as she did so. There was no time like the present to find out.

Jeannie was just getting out of her car when Alexandra pulled up in front of Evan's house. There were already a few cars parked along the side of the drive but Evan's sister spotted Alexandra and waited for her.

"I wanted to get here early but the baby was fussy and this is the first time I've left her and my husband called at the last minute and said he was tied up with an appointment and would have to meet me here and everything was just a last-minute mess," she offered all in one breath as they crossed the courtyard together.

Alexandra laughed at the outpouring, grateful for the casual familiarity it offered. "I'm sure the party will be perfect anyway."

Jeannie didn't bother to ring the bell—just went in the front door as if the house were hers. A man Alexandra didn't recognize took their coats and they went in search of Evan.

They found him with a small group of guests in the collection room. Excusing himself, he crossed to Jeannie and Alexandra at the doorway. But his eyes were only on Alexandra and he smiled at her as if he'd missed her in the hours since they'd last seen each other. He kissed her, dropped a possessive arm around her shoulders and then turned them both to face Jeannie.

"I hope you didn't race over here," he said to his sister. "Between Mary and all the people you hired, everything is in great shape. In fact, it's been in great shape since an hour before anybody showed up." Then he explained to Alexandra, "She called in a tizzy because she couldn't get here earlier."

Jeannie wrinkled her nose at her brother. "Alexandra already got a taste of my 'tizzy' in the driveway."

"How late will Kevin be, did he say?" Evan asked.

"He should be here anytime." Jeannie glanced around like a harried hostess in spite of Evan's reassurances. "I think I'd better check on things in the kitchen," she said, excusing herself.

A large group of guests came in just then, and Evan bent to peck a kiss near Alexandra's ear. "Would you mind getting yourself a drink while I say hello to these people?"

"No, not at all," she assured him, though when he left she did feel a little naked.

Alexandra found the bar in the corner of the dining room and then took her glass of red wine back into the living room. From a distance she watched Evan. He was dressed in gray slacks and a tweed sport coat over a black shirt. It was a different look for him—something she pictured a new-age artist wearing for the opening of a gallery display—but he looked as good in it as he did in everything else. It was his confidence and being comfortable with himself that made him seem as if he were born into any style of clothes he wore, and Alexandra couldn't help but appreciate the sight of him. But then, she appreciated everything about him:

the way he looked, the sound of his voice, the smell of his skin with or without after-shave, the touch of his hands, the feel of him—everything.

Please don't be like Curtis, she silently prayed as she watched him excuse himself and cross to her again.

"Have I told you how great you look tonight?" he said. He took her hand and kissed the back of it, catching sight of the bracelet she wore. He arched her wrist to study the braided gold strands, complimenting her on it. "Was it a gift from an admirer?"

"Tommy," she replied unenthusiastically, almost afraid to admit it. "He gave it to me when I got married. Marjorie was mad because she'd been with him when he bought it and he had put off getting her something, too." There was no reason to go into all the sordid details except that she was afraid Evan might be wondering if the bracelet was an ill-gotten gain. And maybe he was, because he was still studying it even after her explanation, as if he could tell its origin by looking closely enough. Alexandra bit back the impulse to offer a receipt as proof of purchase.

"Is your grandfather at home tonight?"

Odd question. "No, he and John went to the movies," she answered, feeling a ripple of uneasiness.

Just then Brian joined them, introducing his fiancé Karla. She was a tall blonde with a knock-'em-dead body that made Alexandra feel short and inferior. But the minute the other woman spoke, her warmth put those feelings to rest.

"Karla is an amusement-park freak," Evan explained to Alexandra. Then to Karla he said, "Alexandra's grandfather—"

In the flash of an instant Alexandra thought he was going to say her grandfather was a thief. But of course

that wasn't what he was saying. Instead he was brag-
ging about her connection with the carnival and Tommy's expertise as an escape artist. Belatedly she caught
up with the conversation and answered Karla's questions about carnival life, at the same time mentally
pointing out to herself what a good sign it was that
Evan wasn't ashamed of her background.

Within an hour the house was filled to capacity with
guests. Evan introduced her to so many people that
Alexandra couldn't possibly remember even half their
names and gave up trying.

All of the guests had filed through the buffet line for
dinner and found places to sit and eat when Alexandra
and Evan finally did so. Leading the way to a quiet
corner, Evan whispered that he wanted a few minutes
alone with her.

In spite of his question about Tommy's where-
abouts tonight, there hadn't been any other indication
that this morning's revelations had had any impact at
all on Evan, and somewhere along the way Alexandra
had relaxed. Everything was fine, she thought as they
settled knee to knee on two ottomans.

"There's something I've been wondering about,"
Evan mused as they ate. "With as much grief as the
Breguet watch has caused you and Tommy, I would
have thought one sight of it in the collection would
have made you run the other way rather than take a job
installing the alarm to protect it."

The bite of croissant in her mouth seemed to turn to
sand. She washed it down with a drink of wine and explained the financial pressures that had compelled her
to accept the job. "Besides, the watch is old business.
There was no reason not to take the job," she finished, feeling suddenly defensive.

One of the guests called a question to Evan. After he'd answered it he turned back to Alexandra.

"You know, you're probably right about that mangled letter offering to buy the Breguet not being from your grandfather," he remarked. "It makes sense that he would have said something to me directly when we met."

"True," she agreed. Tommy was definitely on his mind tonight, wasn't he? she realized.

For a few moments they ate in silence before Evan's midnight-blue eyes focused on her, glinting with what looked like secret delight. "I found something of yours under my bed today."

Well, that couldn't have anything to do with Tommy, she thought, knowing right away that Evan must be referring to the bra she hadn't been able to locate this morning. But his grin was so slow and intimate and mischievous, she couldn't resist playing along. Especially when it meant not talking about anything that had to do with her grandfather. "Lint?" she suggested.

"Do you carry your own lint around?"

"Doesn't everybody?"

"This is a little more personal than lint."

"I don't know. Depending on where it comes from, lint can be pretty personal."

"This is underwear," he said in an aside.

"And you're sure it's mine?" she teased.

"Positive. In the first place, no other woman has been in my new bedroom or my new bed. In the second place, I had this vivid memory of taking it off you last night and yet this morning... on the kitchen table... it seemed to be missing."

No, Tommy was definitely not on his mind any-more, she reflected, taking in Evan's quirky smile. She was all too aware of the heat that was radiating from the seductive quality of his voice. "Have you claimed it as a trophy?" she flirted.

"No, I was thinking of returning it—say, tomorrow morning?"

Tempting. Very tempting.

"This party won't go on all night, you know," he coaxed before she could answer.

"I can't," she blurted because it was the only way she could push out the words she'd rather not say. Then she added, "I want to. I really want to. But I have to go home." What she didn't want was to say that she was afraid of leaving Tommy without an alibi the way he would have been last night had it not been for John and the poker game, just in case something like this morn-ing's police questioning came up again.

"Should I sneak away and let the air out of your tires?"

"You wouldn't."

"I might. I might do just about anything to keep you here."

"I really can't," she repeated seriously. Then she changed the subject before having to say more about it. "Look at Brian—he's staring into space as if his dog just died. Is he okay?"

Evan glanced at his old friend. His expression im-mediately sobered and he shook his head. "Money trouble." As they finished their meal he told her the whole story. "I keep trying to help out but he's ada-mantly against it. He gets mad every time I even of-fer."

Their conversation was cut short when Jeannie joined them. She butted her brother over to make room on his ottoman for herself and handed him the latest pictures of the baby. Evan glanced at them and passed them on to Alexandra. They were family snapshots, some taken of Evan holding his niece.

"Ashley loves her uncle Evan already," Jeannie said, craning her neck to see which one Alexandra was staring so intently at. "Look how content she is in his arms and how she's screaming bloody murder in all the rest of these pictures," the other woman pointed out with a laugh.

"I'm just good with women," Evan joked, winking broadly at Alexandra.

A man across the room called to him then, asking for a tour of the collection, and Evan excused himself from Alexandra and his sister.

"I don't think I've ever seen a man so crazy about a baby," she told Jeannie, handing the pictures back.

"He's always been wild for kids. And he's feeling the urge for some of his own a lot these days. I think that's why he's so taken with Ashley."

Was he feeling the yen for fatherhood enough to want kids with a thief's granddaughter? Alexandra wondered as a maid removed her dinner plate.

Dessert and coffee were served then. Jeannie was sidetracked by Mary to attend to something in the kitchen and Alexandra spent the rest of her evening doing more observing than participating in the party.

She was one of the first guests to leave, shortly after eleven. Not that she wasn't enjoying herself. But she was afraid that if she waited too long, until she and Evan were alone, she wouldn't be able to resist spending the night with him. And she needed to resist him.

Not just for the sake of giving Tommy an alibi on the off chance that he should need one again, but for her own sake. She had to put the brakes on her feelings for Evan until she could get a better sense of what he really thought of all he'd learned about her past today. Until she could be sure it was safe.

Evan walked her out to her car, backing her up against the door rather than opening it for her.

"I can't persuade you to stay for a private party later?" he asked, running his hands firmly up and down both her arms.

"Sorry," she said, hoping he attributed her breathlessness to the cold night air.

"Tomorrow, then? As I recall, you owe me a breakfast."

She couldn't help the smile that came in response to the memory of this morning. "I always pay my debts."

"My place or yours?"

Definitely his. "You wouldn't exactly be sitting on your duff if you had to come to my place. And I'll bring my own frying pan since asking for yours just got me into trouble today. Shall I come over about ten?"

He pulled her against him, his hands clasped and riding low on her back. "Will you serve me breakfast in bed?"

"Was that part of the deal?"

"It should have been."

"I'll take it under consideration."

"Do that." He kissed her then—a long, slow, lingering kiss that said he'd forgotten he had a houseful of guests waiting for him.

But Alexandra hadn't. Any more than she'd forgotten that she had to get home and away from this man she wanted more than was good for her. Distance and perspective were what she needed.

She pushed away from the warm honey of his kiss. "You'd better go back in before somebody sends out the cavalry looking for you."

He didn't argue with her. Instead he kissed her once more, briefly this time, and opened her car door for her. "If you can't sleep and get lonely tonight, come back. No matter what time it is."

"You have a cure for insomnia?"

"The best," he answered, his tone and his expression full of insinuation. Then he closed her door and stayed watching her as she wove past all the cars lining both sides of the drive and turned onto the private road.

Maybe she was just imagining negative things, she told herself all the way home.

But even as she pulled into her own driveway she couldn't stop the niggling doubt that was eating away at her hopes for the future. If Tommy's past sins had been so easy for Evan to accept, why hadn't he told her it didn't matter to him? Why hadn't he assured her that he wasn't worried? That he didn't believe there was any problem with his owning the watch that her grandfather had gone to jail for trying to steal? Why hadn't he said something—anything—good or bad?

She couldn't shake her own doubts and worries as she went inside, finding the house still well lit.

"Is that you, Alexandra?" Tommy called from the kitchen.

"It's me."

Tommy sighed so deeply she heard it even before she reached the adjoining door. "I'm glad. I've had a little accident."

That statement and her first sight of bloody paper towels all over the countertop made Alexandra hurry to her grandfather where he stood at the sink. His hand and wrist were wrapped in two dish towels soaked with blood.

"What happened?"

"I was washing a mixing bowl and it slipped out of my hands. My first instinct was to try to catch it, and all I did was slide into the glass as it broke. I'm fine. I just can't seem to get the bleeding to stop."

"Let me see it," she said, finding his left hand and wrist sliced in several places. "You need stitches, Tommy. We have to go to the emergency room right now."

"And leave this mess? Couldn't you clean up while I stand here and then we could go, darling?"

Alexandra rolled her eyes. "I'll clean the mess when we get back," she insisted, taking him by the elbow out to her car.

Chapter Nine

The sounds of Mary and Stan putting the house **back** in order after the past night's party woke Evan Sunday morning. He rolled onto his back in the center of his bed and clamped his hands behind his head, staring up at the ceiling. He could hear muted voices and an occasional muffled laugh pass between the husband and wife working down the hall, and he couldn't help but feel a tinge of envy.

He missed Alexandra and, unlike anyone before her, nothing could fill that void. He wanted her in his house, in his life, on a day-to-day, permanent basis. Realizing that didn't take any great soul-searching, even though it was the first time it had actually occurred to him. It was as if the knowledge that she was the life mate fate intended for him had been there all along just waiting for him to notice it. He loved her. Maybe it had happened fast, but it was no less power-

ful or intense or deeply rooted than feelings that ev-
olved slowly.

And yet . . .

He hated the other thought that had been troubling
him since yesterday morning: she hadn't been totally
honest with him.

Was that a sign of the same kind of deceit he'd found
in Shelline and in Barbara before her? he asked himself as he had so often in the past twenty-four hours.
Was he overlooking something because his feelings for
Alexandra were so strong?

Put yourself in her shoes, he told himself.

Alexandra could have lied to him; she could have
said Tommy had been convicted for one among many
of his burglaries, and she could easily have omitted the
part about the watch. Evan would never have known
the difference.

But she didn't. She may not have volunteered her
history or Tommy's but, unlike Shelline or Barbara,
she hadn't lied to hide it, either. And when the time had
come, she'd told him the truth.

Alexandra was indeed different from the others.

And he loved her.

Now he meant to do something about it.

Evan swung out of bed and headed for the bathroom. But he only made it halfway when a knock on
the bedroom door and Brian's voice stopped him.

"I'm sorry to wake you, Evan," his friend called
through the panel. "But we have a big problem out
here and you'd better know about it right now."

"I'll be there in a second," Evan answered, taking a
detour to pull on a pair of jeans.

He found Brian, Mary and Stan just outside the
open door to the collection room. It didn't take a ge-

nius to guess what had happened, but Brian filled him in the minute Evan came into the room.

"Mary was cleaning up and noticed that the alarm's red 'activated' light was off. She sent Stan for me and I went in. The Breguet is gone."

Evan didn't say anything. He went into the collection room. Not a single thing was out of place or disturbed; every display table or case he passed still held each watch and clock in its proper place. But in the center of the room, the small dome covered an empty pedestal.

"I'll call the police," Brian said from the doorway behind him.

"No." Evan turned from staring at the pedestal to look at his friend.

"What are you going to do?" Brian asked.

"I'm not sure. But I don't want the police in on it. Not if they don't have to be."

"Maybe this is the reason Alexandra left so early last night," Brian mused under his breath.

"She isn't involved," Evan countered sharply.

Brian didn't say anything, but it was obvious from his expression that he thought Evan was wrong to trust Alexandra.

"I don't have time to argue it with you, Brian. But I know she didn't have anything to do with this."

"And her grandfather?"

"He's a different matter altogether."

The first time the doorbell rang it barely penetrated Alexandra's deep sleep. The second time, she thought she was dreaming, but by the third time she was awake enough to know she wasn't. Maybe whoever it was would go away.

When the bell rang for the fourth time she decided she'd better answer it before it woke Tommy in his downstairs bedroom.

"Just a minute!" she called.

She pulled on her white velour robe, zipped it to her chin and forced her eyes open all the way.

As the doorbell continued to ring, Alexandra was beginning to get a little peeved.

"Okay, okay," she muttered as she opened the front door to find Evan standing on her porch looking very, very serious. Somehow, saying good-morning seemed inappropriate, so she pushed on the screen and said, "Hi" a little tentatively. "It isn't past ten already, is it? Did I stand you up for our breakfast date?"

"It's barely eight," he informed her as he came in.

There was nothing angry or threatening in his tone, but somehow the flatness of it was worse. Alexandra closed the door and turned to him. Leaning back on the oak panel, she kept her palms flat against the cold wood. "What's up?" she asked, failing to sound as bright as she'd meant to.

"The Breguet watch is missing. I checked everything and set the alarm a little past midnight last night. Sometime between then and this morning it was taken."

Taken not stolen. He was being very careful how he said this.

"Is anything else missing?" Alexandra asked almost as carefully.

"Not a thing. Nothing was even disturbed. Mary noticed that the alarm wasn't activated this morning when she came in to clean. That's how we discovered it. Apparently the system was turned off without making a peep."

Silence. He didn't say any more. He didn't have to. The unspoken accusation was there in the room with them like a third person. Alexandra's thoughts were racing.

Then, quietly, he said, "I'd rather not bring the police into this."

That gave her a grip on herself. "Tommy didn't do it."

There was that silence again.

"He didn't," she insisted. "He couldn't have. When I got home last night he'd cut his hand and wrist on a broken bowl. I took him to the emergency room but there'd been a bus accident and the place was jammed. We waited until almost five this morning before they stitched him up and there were any number of nurses in and out of his cubicle every few minutes to make sure the compresses were keeping the bleeding down. We didn't get out of there until nearly six this morning."

"The alarm was bypassed without a sound, Alexandra. Nothing else in the room was touched even though there are other watches worth more. How and why would anyone else do this?" he asked, staring at her with those piercing dark blue eyes.

"You think I'm lying?"

"I'm wondering if your grandfather got someone else to do the actual break-in for him."

"I suppose you think he cut himself on purpose, too, so I could take him to the hospital and we'd both have an alibi."

Evan said nothing.

"Tommy didn't have anything to do with stealing your watch," she said more forcefully.

"Come on, Alexandra," Evan urged as if telling her to wake up and smell the coffee.

She swallowed with some difficulty and raised her chin at him. "And if you're so sure my grandfather took the watch, you must think I'm involved, too."

"No, I don't," he replied without hesitation. "Except maybe to have been used behind your back." He glanced in the direction of her briefcase lying open on the coffee table. "I imagine that your grandfather had access to all he needed to know about the system without ever having to say a word to you."

"And you figure he passed the information on to someone else so they could steal the watch for him?" Why did Morty's face pop into her mind?

"What do you think?" Evan asked quietly.

"If someone was going to steal the watch for Tommy, why wouldn't they have taken the rest for themselves?"

"Honor among thieves?"

Alexandra couldn't stand still anymore. She launched herself away from the door and paced. "Tommy didn't do this. He didn't have anything to do with it. He wouldn't."

"I think you'd better talk to him."

"He's asleep. He had a rough night." She glanced at Evan, finding him watching her, waiting. "I don't even know if he knows you have the watch."

"I don't have it anymore. It's time to put the cards on the table with him, Alexandra."

"I will ask him if he knows anything about this—if he might have some idea who would want the watch...."

"You mean besides him."

Alexandra wouldn't answer that. Instead she went on as if he hadn't said anything. "But it's better if I do it alone."

She saw the flash of indecision cross that handsome face of his and it stabbed her. She'd seen that expression before, on Curtis's face every time Tommy's name was mentioned. She had to give Evan credit, though; he looked as if he were trying to fight it.

"What would make you feel better?" she asked. "Do you want to stay up here while I go downstairs to talk to him so he can't disappear with the loot?"

"No, dammit!" Evan jammed a hand through his hair. Then he met her in the center of the room, stopping her pacing by catching both her arms in those big, strong hands that even now made goose bumps pop up along the surface of her skin. "Put yourself in my place for a minute, Alexandra. What would you think?" he demanded with a frown creasing his square brow.

She couldn't help the mirthless laugh that escaped her lips. "I'd think The Great T. C. Dewberry just pulled off a heist of the heirloom watch he wanted back," she replied facetiously, looking up into his eyes, willing him not to be like Curtis. "But it isn't true," she finished with quiet conviction.

"I wish I knew that was true," he said more to himself than to her.

She wanted him to let go of her arms, to enfold her in his and pull her against the hard comfort of his chest. She wanted her head pressed to his heart, she wanted to hear its steady beat. She wanted him to lower his chin to the top of her head and curve his whole body around her like a cocoon.

But of course, none of that was going to happen. She spun out of his grip and away from him, retreating behind Tommy's recliner for protection. "So," she jabbed with her voice. "Do you want to stay up here while I go talk to him?"

Evan just stared at her for a moment, his gaze holding hers as if he were asking her to understand. The trouble was that she did.

Then he shook his head, sighed and straightened just the slightest bit; but it seemed to Alexandra that there was withdrawal in his gesture.

"No. I'll go home and wait to hear from you," he said much too formally.

"Fine."

One of his brows twitched into a momentary frown and he took a step toward her. But something about the way she was standing, staring at him, must have told him she couldn't accept anything from him right now. He stopped.

"I don't believe you had anything to do with this," he told her in a voice that sounded sincere.

"Good, because I didn't," she answered curtly.

"And I don't want it to come between us."

But it *was* between them, as surely as the chair Alexandra stood behind. And they both knew it.

"I'll call you when I've talked to Tommy."

He nodded.

Alexandra watched his broad back as he left, wanting him not to go, wanting none of this to have happened. But it *had* happened and he was convinced her grandfather had caused it, so she stood her ground.

For a long moment after Evan closed the door behind himself she stared at it. She listened to the sound of his car door closing. Of his engine starting. Of him backing out of her driveway. It was hard for her to swallow past the lump in her throat. It was hard for her to move. But she forced herself to do both.

She went through the kitchen to the basement stairs. But two steps down the phone rang and she turned back to answer it on the second ring. It was the woman who had so often called Tommy in the past two weeks, asking again to speak to him. Alexandra didn't get more than a word out before her grandfather picked up the extension.

"I'll take this, darling," he said.

"When you're finished I need to talk to you, Tommy," she told him, wondering where the weakness in her voice had come from.

She hung up but somehow couldn't tear her eyes away from the monitor button on the phone. There was no reason to suspect anything, she told herself. This woman caller was just a lady friend of Tommy's.

But the voice sounded young. It hadn't occurred to her before, but it did now. Too young for Tommy.

Feeling guilty beyond belief, she pushed the monitor button only to have her grandfather's angry voice come into the room.

"What do you mean, the price has gone up?" Tommy demanded.

"Just what I said. The watch will cost you a hundred thousand now."

Like a child reflexively covering her ears so she didn't have to hear something she didn't want to hear, Alexandra pushed the button again to turn it off.

"No, Tommy, no." She closed her eyes and laid her forehead against the receiver as if she could stop her grandfather's conversation that way. He couldn't be involved in this. He just couldn't be. And he wouldn't be. Tommy wouldn't do anything that might put him back in jail. There had to be another explanation. She didn't know what it could possibly be, but she knew there must be something else going on.

Alexandra stood up straight, headed for the basement stairs again and then turned around and went to the coffeepot instead. Strong black coffee. Tommy would need it after only two hours' sleep. Then she put water on for tea and decided she might as well open all the shades so the morning sunshine could come in and take the chill off the house. While she waited for the coffee to brew and her tea to steep she cleaned the mess left from the night before by Tommy's accident. Maybe she should let him go back to sleep, she thought. Maybe she should get into all of this later, after he was rested.

And maybe, in the meantime, it would just go away.

But she could hear her grandfather moving around downstairs and knew he hadn't gone back to bed after his phone call.

So the woman wasn't a lady friend, after all, Alexandra thought. No wonder Tommy had always been in such a rush to answer the phone before Alexandra got to it. Did the woman steal the watch? Why not? Crime was an equal-opportunity employer.

"And I'm a naive idiot," she muttered to herself. Had she really thought that Tommy would accept losing the watch forever? Had she really believed it wasn't her grandfather who wrote that letter from Canon City? Or that he would ever have lost track of his inheritance or who owned it?

But none of those things meant that Tommy had anything to do with the Breguet having been stolen. Even discussing buying it didn't necessarily mean he had arranged the theft.

Or was she still being naive?

Maybe. But she just didn't believe Tommy was involved in the burglary.

Of course, buying stolen goods would put him back in jail anyway; but she couldn't think about that now. She could only hold on to the conviction that her grandfather didn't have anything to do with the theft.

Alexandra took the tea bag out of her water and poured a cup of coffee. Then, with a mug in each hand, she finally made it down the stairs to the basement apartment. Tommy's bedroom door was shut but she could hear him opening and closing drawers as if he were looking for something.

"Tommy?" she called. "I need to talk to you."

He opened the door and went back to searching drawers. "I'm sorry if the phone woke you, darling," he said. "Couldn't go back to sleep, either? I know I'll be sorry for it this afternoon, but I just couldn't stop my mind from spinning after that call." He closed the drawer and opened another. "Somewhere in here I have a sweater with sleeves that have always been too long for me. If I wear it now, it will hide some of these bandages they have my arm mummified in. Ah, here it is."

Alexandra stepped to the side of the dresser as he took his sweater out and set it on top. She held out the mug.

"You've made coffee already?" he asked as he took it.

"I thought you'd need it," she said. Then she took a deep breath for strength. "I was up even before the phone rang. We had a visitor."

Tommy had on his brocade dressing gown, and his silk pajama pants peeked out from below it. He kicked off his leather slippers and perched on his already made bed, his back against the high arch of the mahogany headboard. Apparently he hadn't had any intention of going back to sleep.

Alexandra sat in the overstuffed chair in the corner, hoping that sitting down might slow the pounding of the blood in her temples.

"Who came to visit so early this morning?" he asked when she had trouble finding the words to begin.

"Evan Daniels," she replied, watching for his reaction.

Tommy sipped his coffee and then repeated, "Evan Daniels."

"What's going on, Tommy?"

"What's going on?"

He'd turned into a parrot. Alexandra sipped her tea and forced herself to be patient. "The watch."

"Then you know," he said softly.

"I know that Evan Daniels owns the Breguet. I know he got a letter from Canon City with an offer to buy it." Somehow she couldn't bring herself to say she knew the watch had been stolen last night or that Tommy was discussing buying it this morning.

"I wrote the letter just before my release," he said, sounding pleased with himself.

"Offering sixty thousand dollars for the watch."

Tommy frowned. "He told you that?"

"He told me what he knew. He said the letter was mangled in the mail and all he could make out was the offer for the watch and the postmark—he didn't know your name or much else."

"He most certainly did," Tommy insisted, as affronted as if Alexandra had just called him a liar.

"No, he didn't," she said as her thoughts rushed on. "Do you *have* sixty thousand dollars?"

"Of course, I do. Why would I have made that offer if I didn't?"

"You told me that when you liquidated everything to buy the watch eight years ago you only had thirty thousand."

"And it's been working for me ever since."

"In jail?"

"I placed it with a good broker just before I went in. There wasn't much to spend it on in prison, after all. I knew that when I got out, the Breguet would be worth even more. And I had every intention of being able to buy it."

"You doubled your money in seven years?"

"Actually, I did a little better than double it," he informed her. Then, under his breath to himself he said, "But I didn't turn it into a hundred thousand."

"Why didn't you tell me what you were doing?"

"I wanted it to be a surprise. You're next in line for the watch and I was going to give it to you for Christmas this year."

"So when you didn't hear from Evan about your offer to buy it you decided to use the money to pay someone else to steal the watch? Is that why Morty was around again? Did you arrange something through him?" The questions just seemed to flow out of her in her fear of the worst.

Tommy looked at her as if she'd gone crazy. "Didn't hear from Evan? Paid someone to steal the watch? I don't know where you're getting your information, darling, but it's wrong. And Morty came to talk over old times and take me to see a used car—I told you that."

"Then what's going on, Tommy?"

"Well, for one, your Evan Daniels knows my name, we've been negotiating for the watch for the past two weeks—or at least I've been negotiating with his representative."

"His representative?"

"The woman who just called a little while ago. I assumed he wanted to keep his business dealings with me separate from his personal dealings with you and that's why he was having this woman handle everything, why he didn't say anything to me when we met. It's not unusual, you know, for a transaction like this to be done through a third party."

"Who is the woman?"

"She's never given me her name. She always calls me and identifies herself only as Mr. Daniels's representative. She explained the first time she called that it was an informal arrangement, but that he preferred not dealing with money negotiations himself. Some people are that way, you know—about money. And after this morning's call I can see why he doesn't want to do it face-to-face—we had a tentative agreement and out of the blue he upped the price. Not very gentlemanly of him."

"Tommy, the watch was stolen from Evan's house last night," Alexandra blurted out.

Her grandfather stopped his coffee cup halfway to his mouth.

"That's why Evan was here this morning. That's why I asked if you'd used your money to pay someone to steal it."

Tommy turned his head slightly and looked at her from the corner of his eye. "Are you sure about this, Alexandra?"

"Of course, I'm sure. When he followed me home yesterday and came in on the police questioning you, I had to explain the whole thing to him—including that the watch used to be in our family and that your trying to steal it eight years ago was what sent you to jail. Sometime last night somebody turned off the alarm system, passed up everything else in the collection and took the Breguet. He's convinced you did it. Or at least arranged for the burglary."

Tommy set his mug on the nightstand so hard that coffee sloshed onto the mahogany top. "This is a setup," he said in a tone more forceful than Alexandra had ever heard him use. "I wondered about the coincidence of him showing up in your life, but everything seemed all right so I wrote if off as just that—a coincidence." Tommy got off the bed and began to pace much as Alexandra had earlier, forgetting to put on his slippers.

"So, he mangled the letter and claimed the post office did it? That way he could say he didn't know who it was who made the offer on the watch. But that Canon City postmark would be enough to convict me. And no wonder he's using a go-between. He wouldn't want to chance having contact with me. He was going to sell me the watch through this woman of his, call the police to report it stolen, show my letter to be used as incriminating evidence and then sit back while the police did the rest. I'd go to jail again in the blink of an eye, he'd get the Breguet back *and* keep my money." Tommy spun around on his heel and pointed the index finger of his uninjured hand at Alexandra. "And how perfect to have you install the alarm. The police would think you were in cahoots with me and that's how I broke in so easily. Devious. Very devious."

Alexandra had been listening to her grandfather's tirade while the wheels of her mind were spinning contradictions. Tommy's scenario would make a good TV movie but she couldn't fit Evan into the picture. Evan deviously hatching an intricate plot to swindle an old man out of sixty thousand dollars? She just didn't buy it.

"If that was all true, Tommy, why would he have come here this morning to tell me the watch is missing? That's the dead giveaway. You'd have to be some kind of fool to buy it after that."

"Well, that's the truth, because I wouldn't touch that watch with a ten-foot pole now. He overplayed his hand is what he did, and when his representative calls back at noon that's just what I'm going to tell her," Tommy said victoriously but obviously still without seeing the unlikelihood of his theory.

"He didn't overplay his hand, because whatever is going on is not Evan's doing."

Tommy's tone softened. "I know you care about this man, darling, but don't let your feelings blind you to him. I told you, there are more fish in the sea and the best one hasn't been caught yet."

Alexandra shook her head. "I'm not blinded by my feelings for him, Tommy. I'm telling you that you're right—someone is setting you up. But it isn't Evan."

"Then who is it?"

A good question.

And one Alexandra didn't have an answer for.

Chapter Ten

After persuading Tommy to take a pain pill for his hand and to try to get a little more rest, Alexandra went upstairs and took a quick, cool shower to clear her head.

As she pulled on a pink turtleneck sweater and jeans she tucked into knee-high boots, she began a mental list of possible suspects.

Morty came to mind first and foremost as she brushed and braided her hair.

What if her grandfather had confided in Morty about Evan owning the watch and what Tommy was willing to pay for it? Morty might have seen an opportunity to make a fast sixty thousand dollars.

Alexandra threw her braided hair back over her shoulder and discarded Morty as the thief at the same time. The spindly old man had been a fence—he'd bought and sold stolen merchandise. But he'd never stolen anything himself. Certainly he couldn't have become an adept burglar at this late date.

But he could have the connections to hire someone else to do it; and as Evan had suggested of Tommy, he might even have been able to rifle through Alexandra's information on the system being installed to pass on to the burglar.

There was only one problem with that theory. As sleazy a character as Morty was, Alexandra knew one thing about him: he wouldn't do a thing to send Tommy back to jail. Had he arranged for the burglary, he'd have had more than the Breguet stolen both to detract suspicion from Tommy and to get himself and the burglar more loot.

As easy as it would have been to believe it, she doubted the theft had been arranged by Morty.

Alexandra slipped out the front door, closing it quietly so that it wouldn't wake her grandfather. As she started her car and let the engine warm up she thought about all the people at the party the night before. A crowd like that offered any number of suspects who could have lifted the watch without being noticed. Except that the negotiations having gone on over the past two weeks made it an unlikely possibility—not to mention that Evan had said he'd checked everything before setting the alarm. So it was pretty clear that none of his guests was the thief.

But, what about Mary and her husband? Alexandra wondered as she turned onto the private road that led to Evan's house. They had motive and opportunity. It wouldn't have been difficult for one of them to have watched the code being punched into the alarm so they'd know what it was. Not if Evan hadn't been careful about making them leave the room before activating or deactivating the system—something he hadn't taken as seriously as he should have. And with Stan unemployed for so long now and in need of money, taking one valuable watch out of so many probably would seem like a drop in the bucket for Evan. Not to mention that the woman who'd been calling Tommy as Evan's representative could have been the housekeeper herself.

Still...

The hole in that explanation, Alexandra thought as she turned into Evan's driveway, was that Mary and Stan would have no way of knowing about Tommy and his offer to buy the watch. "Unless they saw the letter before it was mangled," she said to herself as she parked in front of the house.

What if someone had seen Tommy's letter before it was mangled? What if someone had realized the opportunity it presented as a quick and easy way to dispose of a watch they could get their hands on? Wouldn't it seem like a fast way to make themselves sixty thousand dollars? And then couldn't they have mangled the letter themselves and only said it had been delivered that way.

Alexandra sat very still, staring out the windshield at nothing in particular while her thoughts raced only slightly faster than her heart.

She had the answer.

Evan was out with the horses, Mary told her when the housekeeper let her in.

As Alexandra went down the path to the stable, she wondered how best to tell Evan something he wasn't going to want to hear. Something that wasn't going to be easy for him to accept. But the more she thought about it, the more certain she was that she knew who had stolen the watch.

The stable door was open. Alexandra went in without knocking or announcing herself. Evan was brushing Livvy in a stall diagonally across from the door, murmuring to the mare in comforting, low tones.

He caught sight of her almost at once. "I didn't hear you come in," he said, holding the brush away from the horse's hide to look at Alexandra.

"Mary told me you were here."

"Do you mind if I finish up while we talk?"

"No, go ahead," she said, thinking that they couldn't be any more formal if they were in a Victorian parlor.

Evan went back to work, not looking at her. "Did you talk to Tommy already?"

"As soon as you left."

"And?"

For a moment Alexandra's gaze slid down his biceps to his large hand as he plied the brush from rump to thigh again and again. She'd felt his palm follow a similar path on her and the memory was suddenly much too vivid. She swallowed back the answering urge and forced her attention to more pressing matters. "Do you open your own mail, Evan?"

He shot her a curious frown. "That's a strange question."

Not as strange as standing here thinking of what it was like to have those hands of his on her naked skin when there were other, serious issues at stake. "Not really. Just answer it. Do you open your own mail?"

"No, I don't."

"Who does?"

"Brian. He goes through it, throws out the junk so I don't have to be bothered with it; sorts personal from business and gives it to me."

A shiver went up Alexandra's spine. "So he would have seen Tommy's letter before you did."

"Tommy's letter," Evan repeated, stalling the brush as he stared at her. "Then your grandfather admitted to writing it."

"He wrote it."

Evan rounded Livvy's rear and went to work on the horse's other side, his strokes a little faster, a little firmer. "What else did your grandfather have to say?" he asked in a tone that sounded very controlled.

"A lot, as a matter of fact," she informed him, going on to tell him exactly what Tommy had told her.

By the time she was finished, Evan had stopped trying to brush Livvy, stood straight, draped an elbow over the stall wall and was staring at her. "So the story is that he was about to buy the watch from my *representative*?"

"It wasn't a story. It's the truth." But she could see Evan's doubts in his expression. "You know, I could always side with Tommy and believe you're setting him up."

"Except that you know better."

"I also know Tommy's been duped just the same as you have."

Evan didn't say anything to that for a moment, and instead just stared at her, his dark eyes boring into her. "Okay. Then who took the watch? Who knows how hot your grandfather is to own it again?"

Alexandra turned slightly away from Evan and petted the colt's nose. "I think Brian did it," she said quietly.

"Brian?" he nearly shouted.

Alexandra took a deep breath and met his gaze again. "I know it's hard for you to believe, but hear me out. Brian sees your mail before you do. What if he opened Tommy's letter, read it and saw an easy way to make himself a lot of money? All he had to do was get his hands on the watch—which was easy enough since you gave him access to everything. When Tommy was contacted by someone claiming to represent you, he'd think it was on the up-and-up, in answer to his letter. And then Brian would walk away with the cash."

Evan shook his head, staring over his shoulder as he did, so that his face was in profile to her.

It was such a strong profile and she loved it so much. Too much. She tamped down those feelings. "I'm sorry," she said, softly, as if that finished it.

"Why bother to mangle the letter and give it to me at all, then?" Evan demanded suddenly. "Why not just keep it to himself. I'd never have known the difference."

Alexandra kept her voice calm and reasonable, trying not to sound accusatory even though it was an accusation she was leveling. "Because by giving you the letter instead of keeping it to himself, he left a lead for the police when the watch turned up missing. The police would ask if there had been any unusual interest in the Breguet, you'd show them the mangled letter and suspicion would all be focused on whoever wrote it. If he hadn't given you the letter at all, the list of suspects would have included him. But as it is, that list gets narrowed down to whoever wrote the letter—to Tommy. Don't forget that it was Brian who knew that the zip code on the mangled letter was for Canon City. If the rest of the address was missing when he first saw it, how would he have known that? Unless he took the time to look it up, and why would he? The letter couldn't have been answered just because you knew the city it had been mailed from.''

"Brian is the last person I'd suspect—with or without a letter.''

"He's the first person any of us should have suspected because he knows the code that activates and deactivates the alarm system,'' Alexandra reminded him patiently. "And don't forget that it was Brian who saw my television interview. What if he caught the reference to Tommy? Even if he didn't know anything about my grandfather, the name would have rung a bell if he'd seen the letter before it was mangled and it made him curious enough to look into how we were connected. He could have found out somewhere along the way that Tommy was a convicted thief—making him a perfect scapegoat. Or maybe Brian read the article written about Tommy when he went on trial for stealing the watch eight years ago and he already knew who he was. Either way, the interview would have connected us and been icing on the cake.''

"Brian barely mentioned your company in passing. It wasn't as if he campaigned for me to hire you,'' Evan put in.

"It didn't come to that. He suggested and you agreed. He would only have had to campaign if you'd balked at the idea. And the fact that a convicted thief's granddaughter installed the security system that was bypassed in order to get to the watch would only compound the circumstantial evidence against my grandfather. I think Tommy was right about the plot he came up with, just not the perpetrator—he would have been arrested and sent back to jail, you would have gotten your watch back and Brian would have kept Tommy's money. Money that you yourself said Brian needs.''

Alexandra only realized how fast and loud she'd been talking when she ran out of steam and the ensuing silence filled the room.

Then, very slowly, as if she would understand it better if he enunciated every word, Evan stated, ''Brian is not a thief.''

Alexandra understood how hard it was to believe something ugly of someone close and cared for. ''I know you've been friends a long time,'' she said reasonably. ''Don't you see that in a way this plan protects you. It gets you the watch back. He probably thought of it more as a short-term loan that in the end would benefit him and not hurt you.''

Evan shook his head. ''I've known Brian all my life. He's an honest man. I trust him.''

''He's a man in enough financial trouble to wear his worries to a party.''

Evan sighed and his expression softened, turned compassionate. ''Alexandra, I know you love your grandfather. I know you believe in him, believe everything he tells you. I know you'd do anything to protect him. I admire that. But to accuse Brian of stealing the watch is reaching.''

''It isn't reaching at all,'' she insisted, her voice rising again with her frustration level. ''I know my grandfather, and this was no cover-up story he invented. He was more surprised than you seemed to be that the watch had been stolen. And I can vouch for all the phone calls this woman who says she's your representative has made to him. No one—*no one*—has as strong a motive or as much opportunity as Brian. All the pieces fit.''

"Maybe the woman your grandfather has been talking to on the phone is who he hired to steal the watch. You've made it pretty clear to me how much it means to him. That's a stronger motive than financial problems that I'd bail Brian out of at the drop of a hat."

"Except that you said he won't take your help."

"If the trouble was bad enough, he'd take my help before he'd steal from me."

"Unless he really thought he was only borrowing from you."

Evan didn't even waver. He just looked as if he were sorry for her.

"Tommy didn't do it," she stated once more—strongly, flatly, as firmly as he had defended his friend. "And he wasn't involved with whatever did happen. But I know that no matter how many times I say it, you're not going to be convinced he's innocent unless we prove it to you."

One of his eyebrows arched. "How would you do that?"

"I think I can persuade Tommy to arrange with the go-between to bring the watch for him to see—he can claim he wants to make sure it's really his before agreeing to the increase in the price. After he sees it he can say he needs some time to raise the additional money, and walk away. You and I can be watching this whole thing from a distance. Maybe you'll recognize the woman who's been negotiating this. If not, we can follow her and keep watching her until Brian shows up or she goes to him."

"What are you thinking now? That Karla is the go-between?" he asked, as if this made her theory all the more ridiculous.

Alexandra looked him straight in the eye. "I think anything is possible."

"Except that you grandfather is responsible for the disappearance of the watch."

"I know that isn't possible."

She saw him take a deep breath and hold it. He closed his eyes and she had the feeling that he was trying to find a way to make her be reasonable. Then he sighed and looked at her again. "Playing cloak and dagger is crazy."

"Do you have a better idea?" Alexandra challenged.

"Was this your grandfather's plan? Maybe it's a ruse to make him look good, to clear himself by turning over whoever it is he had steal the watch."

"It didn't even occur to me that Brian is the most likely suspect until I pulled into your driveway. I just thought of this plan a few minutes ago. Tommy doesn't know anything about any of it," she said heatedly, losing her patience. "If you're so sure Brian didn't do it, what's the harm?"

"The harm is in giving Tommy...or whoever has the watch...more time to hide it."

Alexandra's arms shot up into the air. "Fine. Then call the police. Tommy and I have an ironclad alibi for last night. He won't go near that watch, so there's no way to pin the burglary or anything to do with it on him. The whole thing can be handled by the police and you'll be left wondering what Brian is going to take next. And you still won't have your watch back."

Evan held his hands up, one of them with the grooming brush in it, the other, palm outward. "Okay, okay." He threw the brush into an empty bucket at the back of the stall, overturning it with the toss. "Set up the meeting. But I'm going on record as saying I don't believe Brian is the thief.''

''You won't tip him off, will you?''

''If I'm going to go through with trying to trap whoever took the watch, telling anybody about it would be a little silly, wouldn't it?''

''All right, then. I'll go and do what I can to get Tommy to agree.'' As Alexandra took a step away from where she'd been standing, Evan reached out and caught her wrist before she could go any farther.

''Not yet,'' he said.

He pulled her into his arms, against his body, just the way she'd been wanting him to earlier this morning. Alexandra told herself to resist both him and her own needs and feelings for him the way she had then, but now she couldn't. She didn't want to. Anger, frustration, worry—none of it was a match for what she felt for him, for the need to find comfort in his arms in spite of the fact that they were on opposite sides of the situation and the suspicions.

''This is outside of us, Alexandra,'' he spoke into her hair, his breath warm on her scalp. ''We're involved in it, caught up in it, but it doesn't have anything to do with what's between us.''

Funny, she'd said something much like that to Curtis not long after Tommy had been arrested eight years ago. She'd been wrong. But, for this moment, she needed Evan's big body wrapped around hers. She needed his strong, powerful arms holding her. She needed the sound of his heartbeat in her ear, the smell of his after-shave, the feel of his chin on the top of her head, of his firm chest beneath her cheek.

''I love you,'' Evan said, then.

"I love you, too," she answered, closing her eyes as if that would block out everything else.

"Your grandfather isn't a part of that."

But he is a part of me, she couldn't help thinking. "Don't talk," she said, because his words made it harder for her to accept what she craved from him.

He tipped up her chin with a single finger and looked into her eyes. "It's going to be okay," he assured her, before lowering his mouth to hers.

His lips were parted, warm, familiar now. The kiss was comforting, as if it confirmed what he'd said about this mess with the watch being outside of what was between them. In fact, for that moment she even believed it.

She wrapped her arms around him, finding the steely expanse of his back reassuring. His tongue met hers and coaxed it to play as he slipped his hands underneath her sweater to the bare skin at the base of her spine. He pulled her so close her body melded into his in that perfect fit she'd recognized when they'd made love.

Everything would be all right, she thought, finding the bottom of his sweater to slide her hands underneath, too.

His skin was so warm and smooth. Muscles rippled under her palms and at her hips she felt his response in the hard ridge that pushed his jeans against hers.

Her breasts were pressed into his chest and yearning for the touch of his hands, the hot velvet of his mouth. Lower, much lower, another part of her body cried out for him.

But the complicated situation they were locked in wasn't too far from Alexandra's mind even now, and she realized that as much as she wanted him to make love to her right there on the stable floor, she couldn't.

She ended the kiss and held a deep breath, hoping it might help extinguish the fires of her flesh. "I have to go. It won't be easy to talk Tommy into cooperating, and everything will have to be arranged."

Evan nodded, ducked in for another brief kiss and then pulled his hands out from under her sweater to drape an arm across her shoulders and walk her around the house to her car.

"Tommy said the go-between was supposed to call again around noon. He mustn't know how to contact her, so we don't want to miss it," she explained along the way, not wanting to add that if Tommy got the call before Alexandra had a chance to talk to him, her grandfather was going to give the woman a taste of what he thought of Evan and end all negotiations. "I'll let you know as soon as he talks to her."

Evan opened the car door for her, leaning over it once she'd gotten behind the wheel. "I'll be waiting," he said, sounding a little sad, as if he thought she had a rude awakening coming.

She started her engine. He closed the door and waved, his smile sympathetic as she drove off.

That parting expression, the sad sound of his voice, stayed with her. "Tommy didn't do it," she said out loud, her certainty of it in her tone, as if Evan could still hear her.

And all the way home she wondered how just being taken in Evan's arms could have made her forget what he thought of her grandfather.

"I don't like it, Alexandra," Tommy announced when she'd explained her plan to expose the real thief.

"We could be walking into a trap. Evan Daniels could have the police waiting to nab me the minute I get within ten feet of the watch."

Alexandra prayed for patience. Defend Tommy to Evan, defend Evan to Tommy—she was being pulled from both ends. "What would that accomplish?" she asked, glancing at the clock and noting that it was a quarter to twelve. "If Evan really was in on some plot to swindle you out of your money, having you sent to jail wouldn't accomplish anything. Or do you think, now, that he's just trying to have you put back in prison for the fun of it?"

"Why should we help him find out who really stole the watch?" her grandfather argued. "Let him and the police do that."

"If the police are brought in on it you know you're going to be the first one they question. And when they find out about your calls from this woman, it'll look even worse for you. They could claim that you conspired with her to commit a crime or intended to knowingly buy stolen goods. And either way, you'd be in deep trouble again. Is that what you want?"

Tommy frowned at her, screwing up his face and squinting his eyes in the process. "I don't like it, darling. I just don't like it. It's a messy business. And you could be putting yourself right in the midst of some seriously bad characters. I won't have you in danger."

"There's no danger," she nearly shouted for the third time. This argument was going around in circles.

The phone rang just then, and they stared at each other.

"It's the only way, Tommy," she whispered, as if the caller could hear her. "Please."

Tommy pursed his lips and turned his head just enough to leave him scowling at her from the corners of his eyes. Then he went to answer the phone and Alexandra followed him, standing right beside him as he said hello.

He stared at her as the caller spoke and then sighed. "I want to see it," he said into the receiver. "I'll have to make sure it's my watch before we take this any further. Once I have, we'll discuss the increase in the price."

The second shiver of the day went up Alexandra's spine. Then she heard Tommy say "No, that won't do. I want to meet in a public place. A very public place. The parking lot at Chubby's Hamburger Palace."

Alexandra smiled at that and it helped some of the pounding in her temples. Chubby's was the only fast-food restaurant with a kitchen Tommy could see from the counter so he could be sure it was spotlessly clean. It was also twenty-fifth on his list of foods he was determined to have once he'd gotten out of jail.

"Eight o'clock," her grandfather agreed and then he hung up. To Alexandra he said, "I hope we know what we're doing."

She smiled at him. "You know what you're doing. You're getting yourself a Chubby's cheeseburger."

Tommy shrugged. "Two birds with one stone, darling. But don't get the idea that I approve of this just because I'll be going into Chubby's afterward for a bite to eat, because I don't."

"You don't have to approve of it, Tommy," she told him, feeling her lack of sleep catching up with her all of sudden. "You just have to do it."

Chapter Eleven

The smell of Chubby's charbroiled burgers greeted them as Evan turned Alexandra's station wagon into the parking lot behind Tommy's newly purchased red convertible. Alexandra had insisted they not drive Evan's car because she was sure the go-between was connected with Brian, and she didn't want Evan's expensive sports coupe to be recognized.

"Tommy will park underneath the sign so the light from it will help us see everything that goes on," Alexandra explained. "If you go around the restaurant we can back into a spot against the fence on the other side of the lot so we'll be in the shadows."

Evan did as she instructed, easing her car between a fluorescent orange Volkswagon Bug and a truck with wheels so big they stood taller than the station wagon's roof. "This must be where the kids who work here park," Evan commented as he stopped the engine.

They could see Tommy's car perfectly from underneath the chassis of the truck. Her grandfather's convertible faced them from several yards away, with its front tires up against the sidewalk that divided the lot and led to the center entrance of the restaurant. The glow of the neon fat boy overhead worked like a spotlight.

Evan opened his window a crack so the glass wouldn't fog, and the scent of the hamburgers became stronger. "Smells good," he said, angling toward Alexandra, who sat more in the middle of the bench seat than on the passenger side.

"They are good. Tommy's favorites. In fact, he's having dinner here while we go chasing crooks."

Evan laid one arm across the back of the seat and stretched out the other so his wrist draped the steering wheel, leaving his hand dangling over it. Alexandra glanced at him as he took in the tiny glass-walled restaurant that sported only two tables besides the counter where most people were picking up their orders to either take out or eat in their cars.

"I've driven past this little dive a hundred times since moving back here. I wondered if it had good food," he said. "Usually these mom-and-pop places are great, but I haven't gotten around to trying this one yet."

Small talk was so safe. "Curtis brought me here the first time. He called it 'slumming' but lowered himself to do it for the food." Tension slipped a derisive edge into her tone—an edge she was usually better at keeping out of it.

"Curtis was your husband," Evan clarified for himself.

"My one and only," she said simply, smoothing the edge.

"And he called this slumming?"

"Mmm. Curtis came from old family money. Generations before him had perfected the attitudes and he was indoctrinated into them from birth. It wasn't that he was a bad person. He just didn't know how to be anything but a snob. It's really sort of a handicap. Very limiting," she mused, keeping her eyes on Tommy's car.

"You don't talk much about your marriage."

"It wasn't much of a marriage, so there isn't much to talk about."

"How long did it last?"

"A little over a year." She tried not to notice how much she liked sitting in the curve of Evan's body or to compare how much better being with him was than it had ever been with Curtis. She couldn't shake the feeling that their relationship had gotten much more complicated in the last two days and that she should be careful not to let her heart get in any deeper. But, for the moment she ignored the warning. "Curtis announced that he wanted a divorce about two weeks after Tommy was sentenced."

"What happened"

Alexandra shrugged, causing her shoulder to bump into his chest. Sparks. How could that simple contact still set off sparks? And in a situation like this?

Then she reminded herself that they were talking about her past—something she shouldn't forget. Evan had asked what had happened to her marriage, hadn't he?

"I didn't tell Curtis about my carnival background before we were married. I'd had too much experience with how it turned people off. But of course no one can be around Tommy for long without finding out. When

Curtis did, it was a blow to him—more than I'd ever guessed it would be. He said it was all so *seedy and trashy*. I thought he'd get over it, accept it. And me. I thought he loved me enough to eventually just forget it. I think he tried to, too. But he just couldn't. He'd known I wasn't a blue blood before. Later I learned how much even that bothered him. But the carnival stuff was too much. It was as if he suddenly saw me in a different light. He lived in fear that Tommy would say something and everyone he knew would find out."

She glanced at Evan and found him shaking his head. "Dumb."

"Anyway, that was the first big crack in the marriage. A month after that, Tommy was arrested for stealing the watch. The article came out linking him to burglaries all over the country and it publicly spilled the beans about the carnival. Curtis's family, friends, business associates—everybody read the whole story. It was as hard on Curtis in that respect as it was on me to find out Tommy had been stealing money to keep my grandmother in the nursing home all those years."

"But you couldn't divorce Tommy."

"I wouldn't have even if I could have," she said pointedly. "Curtis tried to tough it out. He even paid my grandfather's bail and got him a good lawyer who managed to keep Tommy from having to stay in jail until the trial. The whole process—hearings, court dates, the trial itself and then the sentencing—took almost a year."

"And Curtis stuck by you through the whole thing?"

"Well, not really. I mean, he paid for the lawyer but then he washed his hands of it. He wanted me to distance myself, too. Which, of course, I couldn't do. And he certainly didn't want my grandfather included in our life. All the while Tommy was out on bond Curtis had a fit if I let him come to the house or invited him to any family functions—holidays, anything. He was sure Tommy wouldn't be able to resist stealing a treasure or two.'' Her voice trailed off as if she'd said something she shouldn't have. She pressed her palms together and stuck her hands between her knees.

"Cold?" Evan asked, clasping the back of her neck and squeezing with just enough pressure to let her know he cared.

"No, I'm fine." She almost said "just nervous" but caught herself. Curtis would have construed that as worry that Tommy really was guilty. Maybe Evan would, too.

He curved his arm around her neck and blew on his hand. "I'm freezing even if you're not. When did you say this woman was supposed to show up here?"

"Eight." Alexandra checked the clock on the dashboard. It was eight-fifteen. "She'll be here. She couldn't have gotten suspicious and not come. Tommy didn't say anything to give this away." And now she was defending him even when there wasn't an accusation. Not good.

Evan uncurled his arm from around her neck and rubbed her elbow, more a gesture of comfort than an attempt to warm them up. He was watching her, she could feel it. What was he looking for?

She glanced at him from the corner of her eye and that was all it took to give her the answer. There was an expression of sympathy on his face again. And he was sitting there so patiently, as if he knew how this was all going to play out and he were just humoring her until she accepted the worst of Tommy.

But before she could say anything a white sedan pulled into the parking lot, stopped directly behind Tommy's car to block him from backing out.

"Is that her?" Alexandra asked, sitting up straight, away from the seat to get a better look as a woman got out of the car and went to Tommy's window.

How did she know which car was Tommy's? Alexandra wondered. Had Tommy told her what kind of car he'd be in? He hadn't. He hadn't said anything about how they would know each other. Unless he'd talked to her again when Alexandra had napped this afternoon. But why would he have?

"That must be the go-between," she said of the obvious as they watched her grandfather roll down his window. "Do you know her?"

Evan leaned forward far enough to see past Alexandra. "No. Do you?"

The woman was tall and slim, dressed in blue jeans and a car coat. Her hair was short and blond, her features—as far as Alexandra could tell—were plain. "She's no one I recognize," Alexandra answered when she was sure.

"It isn't Karla," Evan pointed out.

"I know. I met Brian's fiancée at your party," she said a little peevishly, thinking Evan must feel that vindicated his friend and put the suspicion back on Tommy.

The woman opened her big purse, then, and handed Tommy a plain brown lunch bag. It disappeared into the car for only a few minutes before Tommy returned it.

"The joke would be on us if she gave him the watch and what he just passed back was something else," Evan said more to himself than to her.

Just then the woman got back into the sedan she'd left running and put her seat belt on.

"Start the car, she's leaving!" Alexandra nearly shouted.

They had followed Tommy into the entrance of the parking lot. The driveway on their side was the exit. The sedan rounded the building, passed directly in front of them and stopped only for a moment before turning onto Youngsfield.

Though he'd pulled up right behind her at the curb, traffic kept Evan from immediately following her out of Chubby's parking lot. And then, even when Evan could have made it a moment later, he didn't.

"Go, go!" Alexandra shot him a look and found him staring into the rearview mirror instead of watching for a break in traffic. Glancing over her shoulder she saw what he was looking at—Tommy locking his little car and heading for Chubby's. Evan was debating with himself. It was as clear to her as if he'd said it. He was wondering if he was about to be led on a false chase while Tommy got away with the watch. But Alexandra didn't have time to argue it anymore. "Go before we lose her!"

With a last look in the mirror as if he weren't sure he was doing the right thing, Evan pulled onto Youngsfield. Luckily the white sedan was only two cars ahead of them, stopped at a red light.

Alexandra fought the urge to defend Tommy yet again and instead kept one hand on the dashboard, leaning forward as if that would keep the sedan in sight.

Maintaining his distance even after the two cars that separated them had turned off, Evan followed the go-between north a few miles before she turned left, taking the same path Alexandra traveled to get to her own house. For one crazy moment Alexandra pictured the woman leading them there, but then they passed Alexandra's street, turning left instead of right four blocks farther east. The distance between them closed fast when the sedan barely rounded the corner and instantly pulled into the driveway of the second house, a white stucco.

"Watch where she goes. I'll have to drive past so she doesn't recognize we're following her, and double back."

As if Alexandra had to be told not to take her eyes off the white sedan. Sitting up as rigidly as a steel pipe, she pivoted in the seat and kept her eyes trained on the woman as she got out of the car and headed for the house.

"Turn off the lights and make a U. She's going in."

The street was poorly lit and narrow. And with their headlights gone it was hard to maneuver the station wagon around safely. By the time they made it back to the white stucco, the front door was closed.

Evan pulled over to the curb in front of the house next door and turned off the engine. There was a large picture window at the front of the stucco showing yellow light through a drawn shade. And against the shade was the silhouette of a man.

"Brian's there!" Alexandra said victoriously.

"You can't tell that it's Brian from a shadow."

"Well, whoever it is is a big man, and it's not Tommy."

"Do you know the house?"

"No. Do you?" Alexandra shot back defensively.

"No, I don't. I also don't see any other car."

"Maybe it's in the garage."

"Maybe we should call the police," Evan suggested reasonably.

Alexandra tore her eyes away from the picture window where the silhouette of the woman had joined the man's. She looked at Evan. "I know you don't want to believe that's Brian in there, but pretend for just a second that it might be. Bringing the police in will raise a lot of questions—some of them directed at Tommy, yes. But if the police go into that house and find your friend with your missing watch, it will be all wrapped up for Brian. Is that what you want?"

"It isn't Brian."

"Then call the police."

There was silence in the car for a moment before Evan replied, "Do you have a plan for getting in there ourselves? We can't just ring the doorbell and expect to be invited in."

"Maybe we could get them to come out here—then we'd see who the man is."

There was another moment of silence before Evan sighed. "Keep your fingers crossed that your go-between didn't lock her car," he said as he opened his door and got out.

Alexandra didn't waste any time following him. "What are you going to do?" she whispered.

In the moonlight she saw him raise an eyebrow her way just before he snapped off a low branch on a tree that bordered the property. "I'm going to get them out here."

Both figures had moved away from the window by the time Evan and Alexandra reached the white sedan at the driveway. Evan eased the passenger door open. The first thing he did was turn off the interior light. Then he crawled across the seat with the branch, wedging it into the steering wheel, so the horn went off and continued to blare unceasingly into the evening stillness. Quickly he pushed himself out again, closed the door quietly and hunched down, pulling Alexandra with him.

The porch light went on, casting a brighter glow into the shadows of the night. The scream of the horn drowned out all other sounds until the door on the driver's side of the car opened.

That was when Evan stood and Alexandra joined him a split second later.

"Oh, my God!" she whispered into the sudden silence when the branch had been pulled away from the steering wheel.

Evan's arm went around her as if he thought she might lose her balance, but Alexandra knew there was no chance of that. She was frozen stiff.

"John."

Startled, her old friend looked as surprised as Alexandra sounded. Then he must have realized what was happening because he couldn't meet her eyes. He dropped his head back and swore up at the stars.

"You took the watch?" Alexandra said, hardly able to believe it even though she was face-to-face with the fact. "You set Tommy up?"

He drew his head erect and then lowered it to stare down at the ground, once more uttering a foul epithet, apparently having no intention of answering Alexandra's questions.

"We could just call the police," Evan threatened, his deep voice sounding authoritative. "Or, we could step inside and you could tell us what the hell is going on. Your choice."

John swore yet again and turned on his heel as if that were the only thing he had to say for himself.

Alexandra took it as acquiescence and followed him into the house as she might have done any other time, still trying to absorb what was going on.

Inside the Spanish-style home the brown paper sack the go-between had passed to Tommy was on the coffee table as carelessly as if it were an uneaten lunch.

"That horn was enough to wake the dead," the woman said as she came into the living room from the kitchen, wiping her hands on a dish towel. Seeing Alexandra and Evan brought her up short. She shot a glance from them to the paper bag and then to John, who shook his head fatalistically.

"The old man must have caught on," John told the woman Alexandra assumed was Marissa.

The derision in his tone when he referred to Tommy lit the fuse of anger in Alexandra and launched her out of her stupor. "*The old man* didn't catch on. We followed your girlfriend from Chubby's." She looked at the go-between. "This is Marissa, isn't it?"

"Yeah," John admitted without looking at either woman.

Alexandra picked up the paper sack and opened it, taking out the Breguet. She barely glanced at it, running a thumb over the notches that marked it as Tommy's. Then she handed it to Evan, wadded up the bag and threw it at her old friend, hitting him squarely in the chest. "Why would you do something like this?" she demanded, her voice cracking slightly. "Why would you do it to Tommy, of all people? Or to me?"

John just looked away, still obviously reluctant to say anything.

"Maybe the police can get him to talk," Evan put in.

"Okay, okay," John conceded, shoving his hands into the back pockets of his jeans. "I got tired of never having a piece of the pie, that's why," he said almost under his breath, like a rebellious teenager caught red-handed and yet still belligerent. He pointed his chin at his girlfriend. "I asked Marissa to marry me and she said she would. I wanted to get us started out right and that wasn't going to happen working for somebody else. I needed a business of my own, money to make things nice for her. And I was in other people's big ritzy houses putting in your alarms every day, seeing how much other people have. When the opportunity came up, I took it. That's all."

"And just *how* did the opportunity come up?" Alexandra asked.

Frowning, John turned his head to look over his shoulder rather than at her. "Tommy told me he wrote a letter to Evan Daniels offering sixty-thousand dollars for the watch. He said he'd given Daniels your phone number, told him to contact him at your house, and he was wondering why he hadn't heard anything. Tommy didn't want to tell you because he figured you'd get nervous about him still trying to get the watch back and he wanted to surprise you with it at Christmas. He talked about it every day, wondering why Daniels didn't call, not wanting to call him because if he seemed too eager the price might go up. I just figured Daniels didn't want to sell, but Tommy wouldn't listen to that." John spoke as if he and Alexandra were the only two people in the room. "Then you walked in that Friday and said we had the job installing a system for Evan Daniels's timepiece collection. The coincidence of it was like a sign to me."

''So it was a coincidence that Security Systems was called?'' Alexandra asked.

''A lucky one for me, I figured,'' John grumbled. ''All that weekend I thought about it. I knew I could rig the system so I could bypass it without any problem. I knew Tommy was waiting for a call from Daniels and I knew he'd pay big money for that stupid watch. That's all there was to it.''

''Except that you also knew that once the watch was missing the police would head straight for Tommy, find it and arrest him. Nobody would believe he bought it, he'd go back to jail and you'd be home free.''

He shrugged one shoulder. ''Yeah.''

John—her John—had done this, Alexandra thought. How could that be? She glanced at Marissa. ''And your girlfriend here was only too willing to play the role of Evan's 'representative'.''

The woman's wide-eyed plea to John was admission enough.

Alexandra couldn't help the bitter sigh that shot out of her. She looked at Evan and went on putting the pieces together. ''So, first thing Monday morning the 'representative' started calling Tommy. My poor grandfather just thought you were finally answering his letter.'' Then she turned back to John. ''And no wonder your girlfriend knew which car at Chubby's was Tommy's. Was it her idea or yours to gouge Tommy for more than the sixty thousand?''

''He kept talking about his great investments,'' John said, as if that excused it. ''Telling me I should put some of my wages into stocks, that he'd teach me to buy and when to sell because he'd learned so much about it himself. The more he said, the more I thought maybe he'd made a bigger haul than the sixty. So I told Marissa to up the price of the watch.''

Alexandra felt as if she were going to be sick. ''Tommy was trying to help you and all you could think about was stealing more money from him?''

Color rose from John's neck all the way to his hairline but he didn't answer that. Instead, it was Marissa who piped up. ''It's not like your grandfather is a saint. What about the people he stole from all those years?''

Alexandra ignored the other woman, unable to take her eyes off her old friend. ''I never thought of you. Out of everyone, it didn't even occur to me that you would do anything to hurt Tommy or me. After all this time.''

John looked at her then, not directly, but from under his eyebrows. ''The more involved you got with Daniels here, the easier it was. I thought maybe he'd overlook the missing watch rather than send Tommy back to jail because he liked you. Then everybody'd be happy— Tommy would have his watch back and I'd have the money and you could have Daniels.''

''But if all else failed, at least you'd have had the money,'' Alexandra stabbed. She couldn't do any more than stare at her old friend, as if she might be able to see something in him that would help her believe he'd done this.

After a few moments of silence, John turned to Evan. ''What are you going to do about it?''

''I think that should be up to Alexandra.''

If she could have her way, she thought, she'd close her eyes and all of this would disappear. She'd been so sure it was Brian. How *could* it be John?

"Alexandra?" Evan said as if calling her out of a trance. "Do you want me to call the police and press charges?"

Police. That word reached her. Feeling as if she were fighting her way out of a heavy fog, she managed to focus on Evan and think about that for a moment. Then she said, "As long as you have the watch back I'd rather not call the police. This is going to be hard enough on Tommy without all the questions he'd have to answer if they get into it."

Evan nodded slowly. "It would hurt Security Systems, too. Word would get out and wreak havoc with your business."

An audible sigh came from Marissa and drew Alexandra's attention back to the go-between and then to John again. Alexandra tried to swallow the lump in her throat but failed. It took some effort to talk around it. "I don't want to see you again, John," she said very quietly. "Don't come around anymore." Her eyes stung and the walls seemed to close in on her. She spun around and walked out into the cold night air.

Alexandra was in her car before Evan. He got behind the wheel and turned to her. "Are you okay?"

She nodded. It was the best she could do. And it wasn't true. But he seemed to read her need not to talk at that moment and started the car.

All the way home Alexandra's thoughts ricocheted. John. It was John who had done this. John who could so cold-bloodedly have seen Tommy put back in prison. And Tommy. Poor Tommy who'd been trying to do things honestly and aboveboard, who had taken the blame. Because Evan had certainly blamed him. Right up to the end it hadn't even occurred to Evan that anyone else might have taken the watch. Not once.

Even after seeing the go-between with his own eyes, he'd still thought he might have been witnessing Tommy accepting the stolen Breguet.

She didn't remember the route they took, but Alexandra looked up when Evan pulled into her driveway. The lights in the house were all shining a warm glow that told her Tommy was waiting. Alexandra couldn't make herself get out of the car.

"I'd better tell him by myself," she said.

"I don't think you're up to doing this alone, Alexandra."

"Of course I am," she shot back at him without meaning to.

"All right, then, why don't I wait out here? Afterward we can go back to my place or go somewhere for coffee."

She sat up very straight. "I need to stay with Tommy tonight. I can't tell him this and then just leave him."

But she still didn't move.

Why did her mind hold such a vivid image of Evan hesitating to follow Marissa out of Chubby's parking lot while he stared in his mirror at Tommy? And why hadn't she said something when Evan made that comment about the joke being on him if the go-between was giving Tommy the watch and Tommy was giving her something else in return? Why hadn't she let him know how she felt about that? What she thought of his suspicions of Tommy? She wasn't married to him, after all. Not like she'd been to Curtis. And how had she forgotten some of what it was like to see that distrust of her grandfather in the man she was involved with?

But she remembered now. She remembered a lot of things. She remembered that Tommy was an old man, that he didn't have a lot of years left. She remembered that throughout her life the one person she had always been able to count on, no matter what, was Tommy. She remembered that her grandfather's love for her endured when other men's didn't. That knowledge of his past was all it took to wipe away marriage vows. She remembered that she had to make a choice between Tommy and men who didn't trust him, who couldn't rest if he was in their homes, around their valuables.

"You have your watch back now," she said, surprised by the strength and coldness of her own voice. "It's better if we don't see each other anymore."

"You don't mean that," Evan answered, staring at her as if she'd gone crazy.

"I do mean it."

"Why?"

"It's just for the best. No relationship can survive without trust."

Evan closed his eyes and shook his head. "I do trust you. I realized before I even knew the watch was missing that you weren't like the other two women in my life who had lied and hidden things. You could easily not have told me the real reason Tommy went to jail or about your connection with the watch. But you were honest about it. And if I didn't trust you, would I have come to you the minute I realized the watch was missing? Would I have gone along with this whole thing tonight?"

"And what about Tommy?" she demanded. "You've spent every minute since the watch disappeared thinking he took it. No matter what I said, no matter what other evidence there was, you never stopped thinking he did it—not for one minute." Anger, righteous anger. And indignation. The familiarity of those emotions made her feel so much better than she had since seeing John's face on the other side of the go-between's car.

"You know I can't deny any of that. Yes, I thought Tommy had taken the watch. I had good reason. But you thought Brian had, and I'm not holding that against you."

"It isn't the same. I only suspected Brian because of the evidence. Now that I know it wasn't him, I don't have any reason not to trust him. But you can't say the same thing about Tommy. You were even suspicious of him before the watch disappeared. Last night at your party you wanted to know where he was, as if you were afraid he might sneak in the back door and filch the watch while you were busy with your guests. My grandfather is a convicted thief and you won't forget that. I know. I've been through this once before."

"Don't talk to me about 'before,' dammit. I love you. I want you to marry me."

"Marry you? Oh, no. And I *have* to talk about 'before,' because that's how I know it can't work between us. I know all about what it's like being married to someone who doesn't want Tommy near the crystal or the silver, someone who thinks my grandfather is going to walk off with the ashtrays or anything else he can put in his pocket. I don't have much time left with him, and what I do have I won't spend like that—like I've spent today."

"You told me that the only reason he stole in the first place was to keep your grandmother well cared for. Isn't that true?"

"Of course, it's true."

"And the watch is the only other thing in the world he'd steal?"

"Yes."

"Then, if you're married to me the watch is automatically in the family and I don't have anything to worry about, do I?"

"As if it were that easy. Do you expect me to believe all that distrust can just go away with the wave of a wand?"

"What I expect is for you to see that what happened before doesn't have anything to do with me. I took into consideration that you're a different person from the women in my past. Well, I'm different from the man in yours. Yes, I suspected your grandfather of stealing the watch. Anybody would have. That doesn't mean I won't get past it, that I won't learn to trust him. I love you. I want you in my life. We can work through the rest of it."

She'd said that same thing to Curtis. "I know you believe that. But the trouble is that it isn't true. Every time your pocket change turns up shorter than you thought it was, Tommy will be the first person you suspect. Even in the face of overwhelming evidence that he didn't take the watch, you were still sure he did."

"That's different."

"You may think so now, but it isn't. Once a thief, always a thief—that's what you'd think if anything was missing. I can't live with it. I can't live a life walking on eggshells, feeling as if I have to defend my grandfather at every turn, as if I have to make sure nothing looks as if it weren't aboveboard. It's no different than when I was a kid—seeing the suspicion, thinking I always had to justify everything, feeling as if my hands always had to be in plain sight so there couldn't be any reason at all to suspect the carny transient. I can't live with suspicion and distrust. Not of me. And not of Tommy. I won't.''

Alexandra watched him take a deep breath. When he spoke again she could tell he was trying to inject some calmness into the situation. ''I know that you've had probably the second-greatest shock of your life tonight, Alexandra. I know it's knocked you for a loop and you're in no state of mind to make a decision about anything right now, much less about our relationship or marrying me.''

''What tonight did was prove to me just how much you distrust Tommy—as much, maybe more, than Curtis did. It reminded me of how that tore me apart. Of how it kept me away from my grandfather when he needed me. Tonight is the best time for me to make a decision about our relationship, when this is all so clear and I'm not tempted to overlook it because of the way I feel about you.''

''I love you!'' he shouted, his voice echoing with frustration.

''I love you, too,'' she admitted, reaching for the door handle. ''But it isn't enough.''

And then she got out of the car and ran for the house, ignoring Evan calling her name and ducking inside before he could catch her.

Chapter Twelve

"Chocolate-chip cookies with coconut and maca-damia nuts, hot out of the oven," Tommy an-nounced. Standing in the doorway between the living room and the kitchen he had his fish-head oven mitts on over his brocade dressing gown so he could hold a cookie sheet out as if it were bait on a hook.

Even that didn't make Alexandra smile. "It's al-most one in the morning, Tommy. Isn't it a little late to be baking?"

"You don't sleep at night, anyway. And you don't eat. I thought maybe I could tempt you with fresh-baked cookies so you'd talk to me."

Alexandra was lying on her back on the couch—the spot she'd occupied most often in the past three days since recovering the watch with Evan and ending their relationship. Her life had gone haywire. Food wouldn't go down her throat. She couldn't fall asleep until five or six in the morning, and then once she did, she couldn't wake up until midafternoon.

And even being awake didn't mean she had any energy. She hadn't made it to a single appointment, she hadn't been able to decide who should replace John as foreman of the installation crew, and Tommy had been giving out excuses to cancel everything. Excuses she was going to be red-faced answering for—like the one he'd given Mrs. Canzona about developing a sudden heart condition that had put the whole company on hiatus; although Mrs. Canzona would probably hear the details about the heart condition over dinner Saturday night, since Tommy had ended up asking her on a date.

Tommy set the cookies on the coffee table, using his oven mitts as hot pads. He picked up Alexandra's stocking feet, sat on the couch and set them in his lap. "Two pairs of mountain-climbing socks?" he observed. "You *are* down in the dumps. You only wore one pair through your divorce."

"My feet are cold."

"Always a sure sign of depression with you."

"I think I'm just getting the flu or something," she said for the umpteenth time since Sunday. Too bad she didn't believe it. But the truth was that losing two of the three men who had meant the most to her had hit her like a ton of bricks.

She missed John, missed his shy humor and the feeling she used to have that he would always be there to back her up, to share her problems. But sometime during the last sleepless night she'd come to accept her old friend's betrayal; to accept that he wasn't a part of her life anymore.

Losing Evan, on the other hand, was something else again. That seemed insurmountable.

Tommy pointed his chin at the pan of cookies. "And on top of the socks, I know you're in bad shape when you won't eat one of my special-recipe cookies."

Alexandra sat up, leaving her feet in her grandfather's lap because they were the warmest they'd been in three days. To please him she broke off a small piece of one cookie and ate it. The luscious morsel might as well have been clay for what it tasted like to her, and it was about as easy as clay to swallow past the knot in her throat that never went away. But rather than say that, Alexandra forced a smile and said, "They're great, as always. You haven't lost your touch."

Tommy gave her a look that said she hadn't fooled him. He reached into his pocket and pulled something out of it. Like a magician he held his closed fist in front of her face, then opened it so that a pocket watch dropped to dangle at the end of the chain he held between his fingers.

But it wasn't just any watch. It was the Breguet.

A rush of adrenaline opened Alexandra's eyes wide and shot energy through her. "Tommy—"

"It came by special messenger this afternoon while you were sleeping. Along with a legal paper transferring ownership to me."

"Evan sold it to you, after all?"

"He gave it to me."

"*Gave* it to you?"

"I could hardly believe it myself, so I called him right away. But it's true. He said he'd decided it belonged in our family, that our sentimental attachment went further back than his did, so we had more right to it. I offered to pay him but he wouldn't take it. Generous man."

"I guess so—a sixty-thousand-dollar gift," she said hoarsely as she tried to blink back the sudden tears this gesture had caused to flood into her eyes.

"Actually, it's worth more like seventy-five," Tommy amended. "I just didn't have that much. I was hoping he'd give me a discount for cash." Tommy palmed the watch again and held it at arm's length so he could look at it—he'd die before admitting he needed glasses. Then he put it on the coffee table with the pan of cookies and took an envelope out of the same pocket the watch had come from. "He sent this for you." Tommy tossed it into her lap and went on, "When I called we had a good talk and he invited me over to see the rest of his collection. While I was there—"

"While you were there?" Alexandra cut in.

"Well, of course I went. That's where I was for so long tonight. We had a little brandy, he showed me his timepiece collection and asked me to check out his burglar alarm. Since you made me tell him to have someone else fix what John had rigged, he wasn't sure the other company had done a good job. He wanted my opinion. Anyway, all in all we let bygones be bygones. I liked him better than I did Curtis—thank goodness Evan is different from him. In fact, talking to him was almost as good as talking to John."

That was saying something.

The news about their old friend had been easier for Tommy to accept than it had been for Alexandra. He'd said that he'd lived too long to be greatly surprised by greed cropping up in anyone. But she couldn't count the times in these past three days when her grandfather had said he just didn't know who he was going to have a good man-to-man conversation with now. Morty, he claimed, was a little hard of hearing and, after a while, repeating everything was tiring.

"What did you and Evan talk about?" she asked when curiosity got the better of her.

"His collection, things we have in common like golf and loving Las Vegas and poker. In fact he asked me to a poker game tomorrow night and I think I'll go. Without John to arrange it, I don't know enough people to get a game up myself. We've already planned to play golf next summer, and he's checking into a junket for Vegas next month. Looks like I'll be seeing a lot of Evan Daniels even if you won't," he mused, looking up at the ceiling like a wrinkled cherub.

"You're no good at the innocent role, Tommy. If you have something to say, say it."

He closed his eyes and raised his brows loftily. Then he looked at her again and quit beating around the bush. "I don't know the man well enough to be sure, of course, but I'd say he's in as bad a shape as you are. I'd also say he's going out of his way to make friends with me. I just don't understand this, darling. You obviously love him. He obviously loves you. He wants to marry you. What's the problem?"

How could she tell Tommy that Evan not trusting him was the problem? She couldn't. In all the years of being looked down on because of Tommy's carnival, she hadn't let him see that it bothered her. And not once during the problems with Curtis had she let

Tommy know what was really happening. She had always protected him from knowing that anything he'd ever done had a hurtful effect on her. She wasn't going to stop now.

Alexandra shrugged. "It just didn't work out, Tommy. Relationships are more complicated these days than they used to be."

"Baloney. When two people really love each other they can work out the complications. Well, most of the time, anyway. If you were talking about Curtis, now, I might agree with you. He was a different case. He wouldn't give me the time of day, always so interested in his stock-market report, or his latest toy, or himself. He acted as if he didn't want me around. I was afraid that eventually he wouldn't give you the time of day or want you around, either. But this Evan Daniels is different. I can't believe there's anything he won't do to smooth over the waters between you—not after talking to him and not after him giving me the Breguet. That's some kind of expensive peace offering." Tommy lifted her feet and stood, setting them back on the couch when he was out of the way. "Maybe Evan sent you something in that envelope that'll convince you. But one way or another, darling, think about what you're doing. Nothing that makes you this miserable can be good. And take it from me, I think Evan Daniels is the right one for you." He kissed her on the forehead and went downstairs to bed.

"I wish I could *stop* thinking about what I'm doing," she muttered to herself when Tommy was gone.

Sighing miserably, she pulled her feet underneath her terry-cloth robe and the envelope fell to the floor. Alexandra just stared at it for a moment, wondering if she should open it at all.

But the thought was short-lived, because she couldn't resist.

Inside was a brief handwritten note: "I don't believe your grandfather would do it, but he can steal me blind if he wants to. Nothing is as important to me as you are."

"Now that's definitely different from Curtis," she whispered through the tears that gathered in her throat again.

Alexandra dropped her forehead to her knees.

Different from Curtis.

That was the third time that had been said. Evan had claimed it of himself, Tommy had said it a few minutes ago, and now herself. Maybe the third time made it a charm, because she couldn't stop thinking about it.

Evan really *was* different from Curtis. A lot different. For one thing, his possessions weren't the most important part of his life the way they had been for Curtis, the way they were for a lot of people she'd sold alarms to. Evan took precautions to protect what he owned, but then he went on to enjoy them—even to allow other people to enjoy them the way he had at the housewarming. Another person—Curtis, for one— would never have left the collection room open and the alarm turned off with that many people milling around.

So it wasn't just Tommy whom Curtis had distrusted, she realized for the first time.

Tommy's stealing the watch and his past being exposed had blown up so soon after her marriage and inspired so much evidence of Curtis's distrust that she'd forgotten about the other, smaller things her former husband had done. But she remembered them now; and what had seemed only small things then, now took on a new perspective. Like the fact that everything from barrister bookcases to the keyboard on his computer to the medicine cabinet had locks on them. Or that he insisted Alexandra use those locks and make sure the keys were put out of sight on the day the cleaning lady came—as if it would have been a crime for her to take an aspirin. Or the fact that he left so much earlier than he needed to for work every morning and peppered each evening's conversation with who arrived right at eight, who was five minutes late and who was in extra early and therefore someone to keep an eye on.

Curtis had not been a person who had much faith in any of his fellow men—or women.

On the other hand, Evan hadn't even been anxious to install the backup alarm unit, in spite of the fact that his housekeeper's husband—a man he barely knew— was out of work and might have been tempted by so many valuable timepieces. He wasn't overly concerned with anyone watching over his shoulder to see the combination to the alarm. And he had no problem whatsoever with giving Brian access to everything. Even Alexandra hadn't had access to *everything* of Curtis's.

It was clear that Evan was trying to make friends with Tommy. That was something Curtis hadn't even done before the situation had blown up. Certainly he wouldn't have considered it afterward. And yet Evan had invited her grandfather into his home, into his life, even into his collection room and his poker games.

Evan was giving Tommy a chance—a chance she'd begged Curtis to give her grandfather because she knew no one could get to know Tommy and not realize that he wasn't a common thief.

And Evan had given Tommy the watch.

The Breguet was important to Evan. It was the last gift his father had given him. It was the centerpiece of his collection because it meant more to him than even the things of a much higher monetary value.

Alexandra had to consider Evan's giving Tommy the watch as proof that what he'd written in his note was true. Nothing was as important as she was.

Just the way nothing had been as important to Tommy as Rose.

Evan might not trust Tommy completely, but suddenly Alexandra had confidence that, given time, Evan would come to it. Because the biggest difference between Evan and Curtis was that Evan had the capacity to believe in people—the way he had in Brian. He had the capacity to trust people—the way he had trusted Alexandra even when it might have looked as if she'd helped Tommy bypass the burglar alarm.

And he had the capacity to love people more than possessions.

"It's a good thing," she said, because try as she might, she couldn't deny that she loved him.

So she stopped trying.

She loved him. She loved him more than she'd ever thought she could love anyone. And that was frightening.

Because what if even having the capacity to believe in other people and to trust them, what if even trying hard to overcome his distrust of Tommy, didn't accomplish it for Evan? What if she made the commitment to him, let her feelings be free to blossom and flourish into even more than what they already were and then it turned out the way it had with Curtis?

Seeing all Curtis's suspicions of Tommy, and having him finally say he couldn't go on with their marriage, had hurt. More than hurt. It had nearly wiped her out. If the same thing happened with Evan, whom she loved more even now, it would be worse. Much worse.

"So, what are you going to do, Dunbar? Live without him rather than take the risk?" she asked herself.

But she knew that wasn't really an option. The plain truth was that she loved him too much not to take the risk; not to chance that his capacities for love and trust were enough to make this relationship a better bet than her marriage to Curtis had been.

Besides, she trusted Tommy's judgment to confirm what she felt about Evan—that he was the right one.

And that was all there was to it.

Except that she didn't know how she was going to wait until morning to go to him and tell him.

"It's going to be another one of those nights," Evan grumbled to the ceiling above his bed. Disgusted with himself, he sighed and clasped his hands between the back of his head and the pillow.

Since Sunday he'd had trouble falling asleep. And once he got there it was fitful and restless and filled with dreams that jolted him awake long before dawn— to stay that way until some time in the middle of the next night.

And Alexandra was the reason for it. He was preoccupied by thoughts of her, dreams of her, ideas of how to convince her that he loved her enough to compensate for all the suspicions he'd had of her grandfather.

And Tommy was some grandfather, he thought, his mind wandering as it did every night.

How could anybody not like the old guy? T. C. Dewberry had charm to spare, a terrific sense of humor, crazy stories to tell, and he was more full of life than most twenty-year-olds.

Spending a few hours with Tommy tonight had gone a long way not only in establishing Evan's fondness for Alexandra's grandfather but in persuading him to see why she could be so sure he wouldn't go back to his life of crime. There was a certain integrity about the elderly gentleman that communicated to Evan that dire necessity was the only thing that had, or would ever, cause Tommy to put his talent to illegal use.

Besides, Evan had meant what he'd put in the note to Alexandra this morning. He'd trade everything he owned in the world to have her.

Evan glared at the clock on his night table, sneered at the time and rolled over onto his side. He punched his pillow and then slammed his head down into it.

Sleep, dammit, sleep.

He tried counting sheep. He tried counting each breath he took. He tried concentrating on relaxing every muscle in turn.

And then the burglar alarm went off.

"Whoops."

"Tommy," Alexandra groaned over the burst of noise in the air.

Her grandfather shrugged. "Sorry, darling," he said as he pushed open the door of the lock he'd just picked. "I warned you I wasn't too steady with this bum hand and I didn't know if I'd completely deactivated the alarm."

"You'd better get out of here."

He winked at her. "Good luck." And he jogged back to his little red convertible as Alexandra stepped into the entranceway of Evan's house, hoping he didn't have a brutal method of confronting prowlers.

She got as far as the living room when all the lights came on at once. For a moment she was blinded by them. Then her eyes focused and there stood Evan. Those long feet of his were without so much as slippers; silk pajama bottoms hid his muscular legs, his navel showed above the waistband, his broad chest was bare...

And his face? She hadn't looked at it for fear his expression would be less than welcoming.

Hesitantly, she hazarded a glance. One look at those angular, masculine features could stop her heart. But there was nothing in them that told her whether he was glad to see her or not.

Without saying anything he punched in the code to stop the noise. Then he called the police to tell them not to send a patrol car. When he was finished, he turned to face Alexandra again. One of his eyebrows arched as his eyes took her in from bottom to top, too.

"Black boots, black jeans, black turtleneck, black gloves, your hair underneath a black driving cap—have you given up selling alarms and decided to see if you have any talent as a cat burglar?"

There was too little variance of tone in his voice for Alexandra to know if he was teasing her or being snide. She screwed up her courage and shrugged. "Just this once. I wanted to talk to you, but I didn't want to wait until morning—and you did tell me the night of your party that if I couldn't sleep and got lonely, I could come over no matter what time it was."

"So instead of ringing the doorbell you broke in?"

"Tommy said I was silly to think you wouldn't want to see me or talk to me, but the truth is that after Sunday night... Well, I thought that was possible and I was afraid if I just called or rang the doorbell, you might not give me the time of day." She glanced back at the door, knowing she was rambling but unable to stop it. "So I persuaded Tommy to break in. But he's a little rusty, especially with his hand in bandages...." Her voice trailed off as she turned her head forward again and found Evan standing directly in front of her.

His hair was sleep tousled the way it had been the morning they'd woken up together. One look at it brought a warm rush and then a stab of pain as she wondered if she'd ever get to see it again.

Without warning, Evan reached up and pulled her hat off, watching her hair tumble down around her shoulders.

"What did you want to talk to me about?" he asked, sounding as if he were less interested in what she had to say than in combing his fingers through the length of her hair.

"That you were right. I was a little crazy Sunday night," she answered, thinking that just being this close to him, smelling the lingering scent of his after-shave, seeing the stubble on his chin, were making her a little crazy all over again.

"It took you until now to realize it?"

"It took me until now to realize that you are different from my ex-husband. A lot different. It took me until now to realize that if anyone could get past Tommy's history, it would be you. That with you I could be more important than anything you own."

He shook his head and his expression was so somber that Alexandra was afraid this wasn't going as well as she'd thought a moment before.

"I *can't* be more important than anything you own?" she interpreted quietly.

Again he shook his head. "It's not that you could be. You already *are* more important than anything I own."

"Including the Breguet," she finished for him. "Thanks for giving it to Tommy." She had the same reaction she'd had every time she'd thought about the kindness of Evan's giving her grandfather what meant so much to both men.

Evan tilted his head to look into her eyes. "Tears?"

She denied it with a shake of her head while she forced them back and swallowed the accompanying lump in her throat. "I know the Breguet is special to you," she still managed only in a hoarse whisper.

"I guess you'll have to make it up to me," he said, slipping his hand under the fall of her hair to cup her nape.

"I guess I will," she conceded, regaining her voice. "How?"

She looked up at him, finally finding him smiling that lopsided smile she'd been hoping for. "I was thinking of marrying you—if the offer is still good."

He pressed a warm kiss to her temple. "I think it might be extended," he told her suggestively, his breath warm against her skin.

"That way we kill two birds with one stone: we have one baby who will be both your father's and Tommy's heir and will ultimately inherit the watch."

"Only one baby? I was thinking of a few more than that."

"Well, only one can inherit the Breguet. And in the meantime I can be your own personal protection from theft by The Great T. C. Dewberry."

"How so?"

Alexandra shrugged. "Tommy would never do anything to make me unhappy."

Evan nodded just once. "I believe that. But then I doubted that your grandfather would steal anything from me when we found out John was who had really taken the watch—you just thought I didn't. I believe it even more after talking to him tonight. He's quite a character, and a long way from your run-of-the-mill thief." His tone turned wry. "And just in case you doubt it—I don't think of you as 'carny transients' and I trust you implicitly.

"I believe you." She turned her cheek into his palm. "Although I couldn't blame you if you didn't trust me. You gave me your love, your heart—and look what I did with them."

"You stomped all over them and left me desolate."

She kissed the inside of his wrist. "*'Desolate'*?"

"Mmm. Completely inconsolable."

She laid her hand on his bare pectoral. "I guess I'll have to make that up to you, too."

"No doubt about it. And I'll want some security against you doing it again." He pulled her against him and traced her upper lip with his tongue.

"I can offer security, but it's a little more expensive than an alarm system."

"Oh? What exactly will it cost me?"

"The rest of your life."

"You drive a hard bargain." He pressed himself up against her to show her just how hard. "But it's a deal."

"You don't want to think about it?"

"I haven't been thinking about anything else lately."

Evan raised her face with his hand and lowered his mouth to hers for a few long, wonderful moments. Then he stopped kissing her and smiled instead. "Together *we're* fail-safe."

"We'll have to be, because Tommy thinks you're the right one. And that's hard to find."

"The right one—as opposed to the left one?"

"As opposed to the wrong one."

"It's about time you figured that out." He took her hand and they headed for his bedroom. "I knew you were the right one for me from almost the minute I set eyes on you."

"Almost? Not the exact minute?"

"I had to wait until you turned around— I saw you from behind the first time, if you'll remember."

"That's right. You scared me."

"But I don't anymore," he said as he methodically took her clothes off.

"Well, maybe a little," she answered coyly, doing the same service for him.

"Let's see if I can help you relax, then," he offered, pulling her onto the bed with him.

And then his mouth found hers, his hands began their magic and his thigh rose to the perfect spot between her legs.

It was the right time, and he was without a doubt the right one.

*   *   *   *   *

Silhouette Special Edition

presents

SONNY'S GIRLS

by Emilie Richards, Celeste Hamilton and Erica Spindler

They had been Sonny's girls, irresistibly drawn to the charismatic high school football hero. Ten years later, none could forget the night that changed their lives forever.

In July—
ALL THOSE YEARS AGO by Emilie Richards (SSE #684)
Meredith Robbins had left town in shame. Could she ever banish the past and reach for love again?

In August—
DON'T LOOK BACK by Celeste Hamilton (SSE #690)
Cyndi Saint was Sonny's steady. Ten years later, she remembered only his hurtful parting words....

In September—
LONGER THAN... by Erica Spindler (SSE #696)
Bubbly Jennifer Joyce was everybody's friend. But nobody knew the secret longings she felt for bad boy Ryder Hayes....

SILHOUETTE·INTIMATE·MOMENTS®

IT'S TIME TO MEET
THE MARSHALLS!

In 1986, bestselling author Kristin James wrote A VERY SPECIAL FAVOR for the Silhouette Intimate Moments line. Hero Adam Marshall quickly became a reader favorite, and ever since then, readers have been asking for the stories of his two brothers, Tag and James. At last your prayers have been answered!

In August, look for THE LETTER OF THE LAW (IM #393), James Marshall's story. If you missed youngest brother Tag's story, SALT OF THE EARTH (IM #385), you can order it by following the directions below. And, as our very special favor to you, we'll be reprinting A VERY SPECIAL FAVOR this September. Look for it in special displays wherever you buy books.

Silhouette Books®

FOUR UNIQUE SERIES
FOR EVERY WOMAN YOU ARE...

Silhouette Romance®

Tender, delightful, provocative—stories that capture the laughter, the tears, the *joy* of falling in love. Pure romance...straight from the heart!

SILHOUETTE *Desire*®

Go wild with Desire! Passionate, emotional, sensuous stories of fiery romance. With heroines you'll like and heroes you'll *love*, Silhouette Desire never fails to deliver.

Silhouette Special Edition®

Stories of love and life, these powerful novels are tales that you can identify with—romances with "something special" added in! Silhouette Special Edition is entertainment for the heart.

SILHOUETTE·INTIMATE·MOMENTS®

Enter a world where passions run hot and excitement is the rule. Dramatic, larger-than-life and always compelling—Silhouette Intimate Moments will never let you down.

SGENERIC

WRITTEN IN THE STARS

Love's in Sight!
THROUGH MY EYES
by Helen R. Myers

Dr. Benedict Collier was the perfect
Virgo—poised, confident, always in
control . . . until an accident left him
temporarily blinded. But nurse Jessica
Holden wasn't about to let Ben languish in
his hospital bed. This was her chance to
make Ben open his eyes to the *love* he'd
resisted for years!

THROUGH MY EYES
by Helen R. Myers . . . coming from
Silhouette Romance this September.
It's WRITTEN IN THE STARS!

Silhouette Romance®